Return to Me

Return to Me

a novella

CHERYL KRAMARCZYK

This book is dedicated to all daughters of the King.

May you know how cherished, loved, adored you are,
not based on what you can do for Jesus,
but because of what He has already done for you.

"A wife of noble character who can find?
She is worth far more than rubies."

~Proverbs 31:10~

Chapter 1

Ruby touched the hem of the eyelet curtain, stroking the eggshell fabric with her thumb. She pressed her lips together, tasting her coconut-flavored lip balm. "But do you ever think...?" Her words trembled on her tongue. While rehearsing earlier today the words had come seamlessly. Now she couldn't string a sentence together.

She forced a breath from her mouth and the curtain fluttered in her expelled air. "Do you ever think we're settling when God wants us to do something greater?"

Abe's voice from behind her was honey-sweet. "No. I guess I'm content with where I'm at."

A sneaker squeaked against the hardwood floor and she imagined the tips of his fingers sliding into his back pockets, his shoulders rounding back as he looked at her.

She clasped her hands at her middle, the small stone on her left hand dug into her flesh. She was shaking—but she couldn't let him know that.

Couldn't let him know she wasn't certain about what she was saying. Or why. All she knew was she needed to do this. For herself. For both of them.

She swallowed and turned to face the young man who had been her best friend her whole life, and would always be. "Since I was a little girl I've only done what my parents suggested. What school I go to, who I marry..."

Abe's mouth tightened.

The remaining words of her speech sped from her lips without a chance to reconsider. "And I never asked God what *He* wants me to do. What if we're wrong? What if..." *We aren't supposed to be together?*

She squeezed her fingers. Tight. "What if we're meant for something greater than what we're doing now?"

He pulled his hands from his pockets to cross them at his chest. His head cocked, one eyebrow lowered. "Like a mission trip?"

No, not a...

Her lips parted, words on her tongue. But what if she admitted she didn't love him? If she wasn't sure if he really loved her? That he thought marrying his best friend was the even road because he never had to go on a date, never had to dress to impress?

The spark wasn't there. Had never been.

He looked away. "Missions in Nigeria is a lot greater than youth group, I guess." She noticed his fingertips dig into his biceps.

She wanted to take his hands, to explain herself. All she needed was a little time to explore, to have some time to think. She'd never done that. To think. She'd been so sheltered as her parents' princess she'd never been in want, become accustomed to the security, so much so she was restless.

What was the proverb? Don't ask a fish what it means to be wet. And don't ask her what it means to be loved. That's all she's ever been. And she couldn't feel anything anymore, maybe never had.

"But you have to tell our parents."

Ruby nodded, her tongue as dry as sandpaper. "Of course. I plan on telling my dad after—"

"Today." He moistened his upper lip. *"Before* dinner."

Her eyes locked on his, where an emotion burned below the surface of Abe's molten brown irises. Would he cradle her face in his hands? Give her a kiss that moved planets?

2

Her cheeks heated in anticipation, her breathing quickened.

Why would he? He hadn't before—and she had just broken off a two-year engagement.

She tilted her chin, clamping her mouth shut.

Besides, the mission trip had been *his* bright idea, not hers. She had only considered breaking up with Abe—not of leaving the country.

But as soon as she found the nerve to tell him, he would see her reasoning, that this was better for both of them. Their parents had suggested they marry and they had agreed, but when had they discussed it? Prayed over it? A lifetime together is a long time.

She tossed her straight copper-red locks over her shoulder and exhaled through her nose. "It's not like I'm getting on the plane tomorrow." She crossed her arms over her chest and came to her full height.

"You'll be getting vaccinations for polio and yellow fever, and our parents deserve to know why."

"But I'm not getting vaccinated *tomorrow.*"

"Soon enough. I'll give you the space you want, as much time as you need…" He hesitated, trapping his next words on his tongue. Then, he straightened and peered at her, an edge to his voice. "But it's not fair to keep the mission trip from them."

Her tongue stuck to the roof of her mouth.

She should have just gone and told Abe the truth. That maybe God planned for her to meet someone else, to marry someone who hadn't known her since having their diapers changed side-by-side in the nursery.

How many times had she said she wasn't happy? She jumped at the idea of Nigeria only because it seemed a better alternative than crushing Abe's tender heart. Who knows? Maybe a mission trip was a better plan to listen to God's voice, to learn God's will for her life. Mainly, if she belonged to Abe or to someone else.

Of course, she wouldn't be dating in Nigeria. A mission trip is for—

"Before dinner, Ruby."

Her head shot up. If she had an objection, she wasn't able to voice it. Abe had already left the room.

Abe's legs carried him to a wicker chair on the backyard deck. Stretching his cramped legs, he took a sip of the lemonade, now diluted and lukewarm.

Ruby had always been unsettled, restless even, all through elementary school and into high school. She was constantly looking for the next big challenge, a new project to tackle—but going overseas?

"Do you ever think we're settling when God wants us to do something greater?" What did she mean by that? Because the sorrow in her eyes when she turned to face him conflicted with the question she asked.

Something was off. Would she find what she was looking for in Nigeria? Would traveling to another continent help at all?

His mother stood beside the flowerpot of cherry tomatoes as Ruby's mother, Pam Matthews, collected ripe ones from the trestle, her nervous energy making her fingers tremble on the green leaves. "The website promised to have the perfect recipes for potluck mac 'n' cheese. I don't know though. Velveeta is hard to beat."

But Abe's mother had turned to him, an eyebrow raised. He shrugged and looked away, toward Tom and the spitting grease of hamburgers on the grill.

How would the news hit them? The three people in the whole world who loved Ruby and him the most? Who had prayed for them before either of them had been conceived. Friends in college, who had clung to each other during job loss, infertility, and then when Abe's father had...

Abe leaned back and closed his eyes, both hands surrounding the glass. *Heavenly Father, I need You.*

He wiped his eyes and shot to his feet. Ruby's father would know what to say—except Abe didn't want the news to come from him. If Ruby didn't come out soon, she wouldn't need to say anything. For all he knew, his mother had already guessed from the look on his face that Ruby asked for space. And Tom Matthews depended on God for all matters. No tragedy seemed to surprise him. And Abe needed his godfather's peace right now.

"Hey, Tom."

"Hey there, son."

Abe's palms were slick. Ruby would come out any second—well, she'd better. And although he needed something to squeeze, a glass of lemonade wasn't his first choice.

"Everything all right?"

Abe lifted a shoulder, his eyes darting back to his mother. She should put her glass down too, or else bare feet will be barred from the deck for the rest of the summer.

Of course, Ruby wouldn't know it. She'd be in Nigeria for the better half. Maybe Abe should have let Ruby wait until dessert after all.

The screen door opened and slammed shut. Sandaled shoes slapped the deck and came down the steps. He held his breath, his eyes on the hamburgers Tom flipped on the grill. The char marks swam in Abe's vision.

Father, I need You.

Chapter 2

Abe moistened his bottom lip, his eyes trained on the terminal walkway of incoming foreign flights. His heart kicked up a notch as her exhausted face appeared. Rosy pink cheeks were now hidden behind a glowing tan. Auburn hair, two shades lighter, fell across an indigo shawl he didn't remember her owning before.

Ruby's lips stretched into a smile as her youth group advanced on her. The carry-on forgotten as she hugged the teens.

Abe straightened, uncrossing the leg at the ankle and pushed his shoulder off the wall. Taking a step, he stayed within the shadowed corner of newspaper dispensers and watched. And waited.

Her smile was big enough to crack her face as she tried to clasp each kid in turn. She then turned to retrieve her carry-on, but one of the young men held it upright.

The ache in Abe's gut expanded. Because, as Ruby's entourage whisked her away to the church van, she hadn't scanned the terminal for him. Not once.

Abe pushed his dessert plate several inches away from the table's edge and rested his forearms across the tablecloth.

Ruby's gaze bounced from her parents to his. "And she was a widow herself with two babies in heaven, and she put together this sticky poultice of herbs and I don't know what else." She gestured with her hands. He couldn't help noticing her apple pie slice resembled her dinner: untouched.

"And it smelled awful, but it worked. Whatever it was supposed to do, I couldn't understand her words, but the new mother relaxed almost immediately. Like a miracle."

Ruby's eyes landed on Abe's. Only for a second. He thought she'd settle in his gaze, offer him a smile at least. Maybe take an inhale and relish the smells of her best friend's home. But her attention was grabbed by his mother as she asked a question.

He sat back in the chair and listened as the conversation took on speed again. The babies Ruby helped a group of midwives deliver. The woeful story of more than one infant who didn't survive. On and on.

After another length of time, Abe pushed his chair back. "I'll put on a pot of coffee. Ruby, you brought hibiscus leaves of some kind."

When her eyes flickered to him in acknowledgement, he lifted an eyebrow. "Is it a tea? Do I seep them in hot water or do I—?"

Her expression brightened as she turned to their parents, her face creasing into a smile. "Zobo punch coming right up!"

She rounded the table and followed him into the kitchen. When he handed her the satchel of dried leaves, her eyes didn't lift to make contact. No trace of the exuberant smile she donned a moment ago.

A full week back in the Windy City and tonight was the first time he'd seen her. Oh, he'd stopped by her house on the first day, but she'd been meeting with the activity committee. Who would fling herself into church ministry before she had time to unpack?

Someone who was avoiding him, that's who.

He sank back against the counter, resting both palms along

the edge. "Sounds like you were busy every one of your twenty-eight days abroad."

She nodded as she sprinkled the leaves in a bowl and turned on the faucet to cold, swirling the water with her fingers. The leaves immediately bled a deep purple. Filling the pot, she rinsed the leaves once more.

His arms tightened. *So much for being alone.*

He side-stepped to where she stood by the stove. "I've heard all about your work at the missions, but not a word about you. Any revelation about how God wants to use you? Where he wants you to be?"

"I was pretty busy. Didn't get much time to think."

He squinted at her. *Really?*

What was the point then? And how could every minute of serving in a foreign country not point her to God? Weren't the other midwives believers? Didn't she join a maternity *missions* house for the purpose of telling others about God?

But her eyes were on the knife she withdrew from a drawer and hadn't seen him scowl. Probably better that way.

She peeled ginger and cut the yellow flesh into chunks, tossing them in the pot. "How about you?" She turned to him with a small smile. "Have you met someone?"

"Met someone?" The words slammed in his gut.

Was she kidding? Every day he'd read his Bible and only thought of her. Prayed for his beloved who didn't know herself. Missed her. Counted the days until she'd returned—until she'd return to him.

Chapter 3

A spiral of heat started in Abe's belly, gnawed at his insides. Or maybe it was the ache of desire unrequited. "I love you."

Ruby went to the refrigerator and took an orange from the drawer. "But I'm the only girl you've ever dated. Perhaps someone else would be a better fit." She peeled the skin for zest, orange strips falling to the cutting board.

He stepped closer to her. His cheeks felt hot, the tips of his ears burning. "Did you hear me?"

She cocked her head toward an upper cabinet. "Does your mom have cloves?"

He found a bottle and gave it to her. She sprinkled a bunch into her palm and dropped them into the boiling pot.

"I love you, Ruby. Always have."

She lifted a shoulder. "That's what you say, but—"

"That's what I mean." He touched her shoulders, turning her toward him. He swept a knuckle down her cheek. The electricity shot down his arm, as it always had, ever since he saw her as a woman for the first time when they were sixteen.

A spike of euphoria spiraled across his veins. He loved her. He wanted to spend the rest of his life providing for her, guiding her, protecting her. And he'd wait ten years if that was what she needed to get out of this identity crisis.

He smoothed his palm behind her neck and brushed his lips against hers.

She wriggled out of his grasp to stir the contents of the pot. "I just…"

He slid his fingers in his back pockets, watching her rigid form at the stove. "Go on, Rube. What were you going to say?"

Ruby stood back from the stove, but her eyes lingered on the steam that drifted up and vanished. "The truth is I had lots of time to think. And lots to think about. I loved being in Asana. Jesus is praised for being God, sovereign and good. Full of God's grace." She paused, her bottom lip falling open. "Then the first infant died."

Abe leaned forward. He knew it. Something had happened. God had revealed Himself to her, just as he prayed He would.

"And I thought it was misfortunate. The cruelness of life, that sort of thing. I could hold the woman's hand and let her cry, but I didn't…"

She looked at him then, her eyes soft. An eyebrow descended as it always did when she was being serious. "The baby had died, Abe. And the poor young mom was suffering, not her first failed pregnancy. But I didn't *care.* Not an iota of compassion. Isn't that odd?"

Her eyes drifted off his face. "And there was all this sorrow and struggling to understand God's will—and it should have gotten to me. But it was like my heart was shut off. Abe, that's what happened. And then I thought…"

When her bottom lip quivered, Abe wanted to wrap his arms around her, press her head to his shoulder. But Ruby wasn't the hugging type. And lately she hadn't been the kissing type either, so he stayed put.

Her lips pursed and then her chin lifted. "I need to tell you something."

His eyes stayed on her expression that had gone from crumbling to confident in seconds. That indigo shawl flashed in his mind. Such a shock of color wasn't normal for her and he hadn't seen it since. "What's that?"

"It's what I should have told you before."

His stomach clenched. *Before?* Before leaving for Nigeria? Or before breaking his heart?

She lifted her face. Only a fleeting moment of twisted grief before her composure returned. This time with slanted eyes and lips pulled in. Ready for battle. "I want to date other guys."

A chill wrapped across his shoulders. A blast of ice lined his insides, making it hard to breathe.

Her forehead creased. "Something's wrong with me. Dropping out of college, jumping from one project at church to the next, last week the website, this week summer camp. It doesn't matter the guy or the circumstance—if it's you or my parents or some bereaved mother. I'm not able to love, Abe. Not at all."

She took up the spoon and started stirring. The contents sloshed on the side, spilling onto his mom's spotless stovetop. "What if I'm not supposed to be in a permanent relationship? What if I'm made to always feel restless, and my life will never be settled? Maybe I'm meant to marry ministry?"

So, that was it then. That was it the whole time. She wasn't concerned about finding her identity, but if she was meant to marry. As if marriage would lock her out. That somehow being in a relationship with only one person was a horrible thing. As if marriage was the same as being *shut down.*

Well, he happened to know Ruby couldn't be shut down, couldn't settle. When she wanted to write a skit to teach teens about integrity, he applauded her. Start a Facebook page for Latin American missionaries? Great idea. Go to Nigeria? She had his blessing.

But dating around? If she was concerned about God calling her to a celibate life, what would dating someone else prove?

Unless she wondered if she wasn't meant to marry *him.*

Straightening, he stepped away from the counter. The muscles in his jaw were tight. "What about finding yourself? Asking God if this was all there was, or if you were made for something greater?"

"It's related." She tapped the spoon on the side of the pot. "I figured if I date other guys and feel the same way as I do when I'm with you, then I'll know it's me. Besides…" The corner of her lip inched up. "I'll probably be so repulsed by any other guy I'll be skipping back to you in a few days."

She gave a tiny shrug and her focus returned to the punch. Easy movements to drain the liquid over a sieve, purple liquid filling the bowl. Soft steps to the fridge for the bucket of ice.

His hands fell limp to his sides. It was only a matter of time before his legs gave way too. *Or you'll fall in love and I'll lose you forever.*

Chapter 4

Abe scanned the selection of the banana bunches. Many had green undersides. He'd avoid the brown speckled version.

Why did this have to be so hard? He'd prayed, he committed to wait... But he hadn't counted on the heartache. The longing. Even when she had been on another continent, he hadn't been so worried. So antsy. Like he was trapped in a dark room and he couldn't move to the light switch because of obstacles in his way.

He drew in a breath. *"Your word is a lamp to my feet and a light to my path." Whatever happens, help me to follow close after You.*

He grabbed the nearest bunch and tossed it in the basket at his elbow. Drew in a breath and reprimanded himself for wasting the afternoon. Later today, he'd go to work and—

The air cut from his lungs when Ruby rounded the corner. Her smile lit her face. "Abe! Fancy meeting you here."

His cheeks prickled. Did he succeed in inching his lips up at all? Hard to tell with his face so tight.

"Hi, Ruby."

"It's great to see you." Her hazel eyes danced and she looked over her shoulder. An olive-skinned man with glossy locks falling into his eyes came to her and she entwined her arm in his.

Abe's spine tingled and he straightened his back. *Oh, God, why does this have to be so hard?*

Ruby's eyes were on her Greek god of a boyfriend. "Darian, meet my good friend, Abe."

Abe's stomach cramped. *Jesus, You are the light of the world.* He struck out his hand. "Pleasure to meet you."

The man extended his hand, clamped Abe hard and returned to Ruby's side. His arm now around her, rubbing her back.

Abe's jaw clenched.

"We were just here to buy a carton of ice cream." Ruby looked at Darian, a laugh trickling from her lips. "An accompaniment to the comedy we borrowed from the library."

She mentioned the title. And something else about summer camp registration. But Abe focused on his breathing.

When she ran out of news, he said, "Hey, I gotta run. Hope you guys have fun."

He hightailed for the self-checkout. His mother had sent him out for more than cilantro and bananas, but he couldn't stay and see Ruby being coddled.

In the car he snapped open the glovebox and retrieved his spare Bible. Flipping quickly, he found the beatitudes in Matthew and read until he heard God's voice.

Abe sat back against the seat, letting his eyes fall close. "Father, take my hand and lead me. Because I can't do this on my own."

Abe struck the match and lit the five candles situated among a herd of buttercream rainbow unicorns. "Okay, everyone, on the count of three!"

He led the group of youngsters and adults in a squealing version of "Happy Birthday" and slid the cake in front of the birthday girl. Abe joined in the applause, reveling in the smiles and cheers. Another year celebrated of a life so precious. And how better to celebrate than a pool party?

As the adults ogled over the cake, he stepped to the mother, his palm extended. "May I?"

The woman released a breath and handed over her phone. The group huddled around the cake as Abe took landscape shots. He couldn't contain his grin, even if this was only one of four parties today. Even if the family wouldn't remember his name tomorrow. Life was good. And he was a slice of it.

He chuckled at his own pun, handing over the phone to cut the cake, dishing up the birthday girl first. Soon, her group of friends were consuming cake, and he started slicing chunks for the meandering adults.

The girl's mother came to his side. "Thanks for that. I nearly forgot all about pictures."

"No problem. It's why I'm here." He grinned at her, noting the creaseless forehead, the relaxed smile. *Yep, that's right. I do the work and you enjoy.*

A scream sounded behind him. He glanced over his shoulder at the alligator tears streaming down the birthday girl's face. Her piece of cake had landed upside-down on the floor. Abe brought her another slice, resting his hand on her shoulder. "That piece didn't have enough icing anyway." He winked at her and earned a giggle.

Then he got on his hands and knees with a wad of moist paper towel.

The door of the party room cracked open and his boss leaned in. "Just a sec," he called to her, sweeping the stray crumbs into the dustpan.

He came to the door, paper towel roll still in the crook of his arm. "We still have presents to do."

"I can take care of it." She pressed a hand on his knuckles and her eyes moistened. "But you better go. Ruby was in a car accident."

Chapter 5

The smell of antiseptic burned his nostrils as Abe made his way into the room of the intensive care unit. Ruby's parents were at her bedside, Pam clasping her daughter's hand to her cheek and weeping, Tom standing vigil, his hand on his wife.

Tom noticed Abe first and approached him. "Thanks for coming." The two men hugged and the older man extended the embrace. When he pulled away, Pam, trembling and wilted, came to them.

Abe glanced at the form in the bed. "Any change?"

Pam shook her head, fresh tears cascading down her face.

Abe stepped closer. "Do you know what happened?"

She crumbled against her husband's chest and he held her close. Abe had to strain to hear the man's hushed tone. "Turning left at Schaumburg and Springinsguth. A pick-up ran through the red light."

Abe angled around Ruby's father to catch another glance. Swathed in the overhead light, monitors and IVs on either side of her. A mask over her nose and mouth, her red strands sprawled across the pillow.

In a coma. On life support. Possibly sustaining a brain injury. His mouth turned to cotton as the reality set in.

Tom touched Abe's arm. "Go on. We'll wait outside."

After they left, the only sounds were the steady beeps and drips. He approached Ruby with silent footsteps and sat where her mother had wept over her only daughter. Abe touched her fingers. Her flesh was warm, but a shiver ran down his spine.

His throat was dry and he tried to clear it, to say something, to no avail.

Scooting to the edge of his seat, he took her hand and kissed her knuckles. Releasing a sigh, he retraced his gaze to her face. Pale and motionless, the machines breathing for her.

The door cracked open. At the sight of his mother, Abe let Ruby's hand rest back at her side and sank into his mother's arms. Tears gushed uninhibited on her shoulder and his voice broke. "I can't lose her, Mom. I can't."

Abe squeezed Ruby's hand and adjusted the Bible. His neck ached from the position and he had lost feeling in his hand—but he couldn't let go of her. He wouldn't.

Just as he hadn't been willing to let go of her hand every other day he'd visited her for past month, he wouldn't let go of her now.

"Look at the birds of the air; they do not sow or reap or store away in barns, and yet your heavenly Father feeds them." One of the machines purred. The other beeped melodically, the sound of life. Abe spoke over the hospital din. "Are you not much more valuable than they? Can any of you by worrying add a single hour to your life?"

His throat tightened, but he managed to finish reading the sixth chapter and let the Bible fall closed, the red text giving way to cracked leather.

A tear slid down his cheek as he brought the lifeless hand to his lips and kissed Ruby's dry skin. A lump formed in his throat. "Lord, if it is Your will, may You have mercy and restore Ruby to us. Amen."

He kissed her knuckles again and stood up. Standing close to the bed, he brushed the stray hairs from her temple. "When you wake up, Ruby, I'll be here." He bent over and kissed her forehead.

Tucking the Bible at his elbow, he left the room, taking the stairs, more to get rid of the jitters than to avoid impatience at the elevator.

Tomorrow was the Lord's Day. The summer camp had left without their youth director, but they had more than enough help with all the adult volunteers who stepped in. Without the high schoolers in the front rows on Sundays, the church felt emptier than before. Like the life had been sucked out of the congregation.

Of course, that might have only been him. Probably nothing had changed fundamentally. The sun still rose and set on schedule.

When he was away from the hospital, he counted the minutes until he could return. And with the thirty minutes of reading God's word to Ruby every day, he'd finished all of Genesis. He'd started with Genesis because he couldn't think of anything better, never expecting he'd finish it at the hospital. But he did. And it had become a personal study Abe needed.

He had never before seen how God had been with His creation every step. He had a plan and He was working it out, in His time, according to His will. Even when Abraham and Jacob swayed, God was undeterred.

God was indeed King, sovereign over all. A truth that comforted Abe more than words could tell.

When Abe had decided to read aloud the Gospel of Matthew, his personal favorite book in the Bible, he was surprised to find the theme of Jesus' kingship echoed. Like God was talking to him. Telling him something.

By the time he let himself into the front door of his parents' home, he was drained. A shower was in order and then he'd fall into a restless slumber.

But voices stopped him from retreating up the stairs. He leaned into the living room to see Ruby's parents.

Abe's mother rose to her feet, but her smile was lopsided.

"Abe, let me get some dinner."

"I'm not hungry, thanks though." He stepped into the room, eyeing the couple at the couch. "What's going on?"

Tom met his gaze. "We came to discuss something with you."

The dense tone alerted Abe. His mother remained standing and Abe wondered if he should have let her visit the kitchen after all.

"Son, have a seat," Tom said.

Abe sank into an overstuffed chair, keeping to the edge, his back stiff.

The man looked at his hands and then faced Abe. "The doctors talked to us today and we're considering taking Ruby off of life support."

Abe shot to his feet. "What?" His head whirled and he touched his temple to stop the spinning. "Why would they say that? It's only been a month."

Pam pressed her hand on her husband's thigh, visibly shaken. *She's* shaken? Did they consider what this meant? Why the rush?

Tom, who prayed more than he talked, who had been a father to him after his own died, crested his palm over his wife's. They shared a look and Abe's cheeks heated.

Had they prayed? Did they understand the consequences? Even if they decided to take her off the ventilator only and keep her on fluids, was this their answer to prayer?

Was this God's will, or were they tired? Was Tom tired, and worried about Pam's mental health?

Abe knew about a loved one dying. He knew hospice and saying good-bye. Heck, Tom had been with him! His dad hadn't had a chance—but Ruby? Why so soon? When there was a possibility, when there was hope?

Abe's breath became ragged. "She's still fighting, still—"

"If she hasn't woken up yet, doctors don't think she ever will." Tom ran a hand over his face, his expression torn.

"But she could die!"

19

"This isn't easy for us."

Abe's vision blurred and he rubbed at the strain in his neck muscles. His feet moved on their own, pacing from the window and back. "You can't give up on her."

"I don't want to say good-bye either."

"Not yet." Tears streamed down his cheeks and he held his middle. "Sir, please. Give her a few more weeks."

"I'm sorry, son."

Abe ran from the room, took the stairs two at a time and hurtled onto his bed. The pillow couldn't stifle his scream.

Abe wanted to stay strong for her. He tried to keep the faith. But the Bible lay closed on the end table. Not that he hadn't tried to finish reading the beatitudes. He had. Twice. But tears had filled his eyes on his way to her room and hadn't abated yet.

He brought the chair close to the bed and hunched close to her face. He stroked her cheek, tears clouding his vision. "I love you, Ruby. Always have, always will."

His fingertip circled to her hairline and traced the roots of the strands, now greasy and stringy. A strangled laugh left his lips—even as tears leaked from his eyes. "This isn't the first time you've tried to leave me. But I've held on, haven't I?"

His voice turned gravely, the rawness of his throat from unshed tears stung as he attempted to take a breath. "Ruby, we're running out of time. I need you to wake up. Come on, Ruby. Wake up."

Chapter 6

Abe pulled on the jeans he'd found dumped in a corner. Yanked off the shirt he fell asleep in and replaced it with a fresh shirt from his drawer. Night after tonight, they'd take Ruby off the ventilator.

He went through the motions of scrubbing his teeth. He would have kept the whiskers, but then his mother would worry. He'd seen the number for the therapist on the fridge, and as much as he needed it, he wanted to spend every minute possible at Ruby's side.

Was Ruby listening? Could she hear his desperate pleas? And if she could, would Ruby return to him? Would she want to return to him?

He'd worry about their relationship later. First, Ruby had to live.

He patted his smooth cheeks dry when footsteps sounded on the stairs. His mother stopped at the bathroom, breathless. "She's awake."

Stars danced in his eyes. He couldn't feel the towel in his fingers until it landed on his bare feet. His heart raced, matching his shallow breaths.

He shoved his feet in shoes and bolted to the back seat of the Matthews's car.

A gray mist. Shadows hovered. Muffled voices.

Floating. Her arms were weightless. She couldn't feel her toes. Disjointed limbs drifting on a ribbon of air.

A woman's voice. But even though she strained, she couldn't make out the words. The sound came closer.

"We missed you…"

She fought to stay awake. To listen.

"…love you…waiting…"

Foggy. Her head was cotton. *Stay awake.*

But the darkness overtook her, folding her within its dense blankets. Carried her deep. Warmth surrounded her, crossed her heart, bound her chest in a close embrace.

Softness and warmth smoothed the back of her hand. Enclosing her fingers, squeezing gently.

A rustling beside her. She forced her eyes open. White as lightning burned her eyes. She squeezed her eyes shut, turning her face away.

The darkness beckoned. Promised her rest. No more harsh light. No more straining.

"It's me."

A soft voice. Sweet as honey. She focused on the touch, the heat against her flesh.

It took all her strength to concentrate. To clear the cotton from her head to focus on the words that drifted to her ears.

"Everything's all right now. Just rest."

The pressure behind her eyes released. Her body gave way to the tug. The wisps of shadows danced until they settled over her as a tent.

Warmth. Darkness. Silence…

"I love you, Ruby." A moist touch on her forehead before she surrendered to the deep.

Abe shucked the sports coat to a hook at the entry way and shrugged out of his button-down shirt. He tried to postpone

---

the interview, but his mother—and the Holy Spirit's prompting from God's word—wouldn't let him.

But that didn't mean he was going to miss any more time with Ruby.

She'd been drowsy for the better part of the week as they pumped her with morphine to keep her comfortable. Because she clearly wasn't.

She could hardly open her eyes most days—but she was awake! And he wasn't going to let nay-saying doctors or good-intentioned parents dampen his good mood. God's got this. And Abe was determined to keep her status in God's hand until the end.

The drive was clogged with evening traffic. Ruby's parents called to say she had been awake enough today to talk—to *talk!* They said they'd stay with her until he arrived, but if a twenty-minute drive became forty minutes he wouldn't be surprised if they'd left to get some rest.

But, no, nothing—not even the maniac Chevrolet that cut him off—could deter him from what he had come to believe. What he had come to realize about God, even if he struggled to remember when the pain of losing Ruby had become too much: that Jesus was King. Jesus had all authority.

For the past decade since meeting God, Abe's relationship to Him had been as his Everlasting Father, his protector, the one who loved him, and would guide him. But now to believe in God who was the one with supreme control over life and death, the one with the ultimate say, had brought Abe to a new level of faith.

And even if something horrible had happened, even if the week had ended and Ruby's parents consented to taking away the air from her lungs, God would still be King. It would be tough, but death was not the end. God would still earn all the glory.

His chest warmed. Praise Jesus. God had mercy on him. Sweet mercy. God had returned his Ruby to him.

Abe couldn't smother the smile as he waited for the

visitor's pass. As he shot up the stairs, his heart pounding to the tune of a rock band.

He spied Ruby's parents as they met him outside Ruby's hospital room.

"Pam, Tom, good to see you. Visiting hours are nearly over, so I gotta rush."

Pam touched his arm. "There's something we have to tell you."

"Sure." He hardly glanced at her, his attention pulled to the door as a nurse entered. "What is it?"

"She can't remember."

Abe looked at Pam.

The woman pressed her lips together, her fingertips digging into his bicep. "Not her name, her birth date. Not us or..." Her voice trailed as if she was about to mention something else.

Abe pursed his lips. *No nay-saying.* "Then we'll remind her."

He slid out of her grip and dodged for the doorway, left ajar by the nurse.

The lights were on. He'd never noticed the color of the walls before. A pale shade of green. Earthy, calming. He smiled and approached the bed. The nurse was taking her blood pressure and Ruby was watching her.

"She can't remember."

And what Pam wanted to warn him about was that Ruby couldn't remember *him.* Couldn't remember being next-door neighbors their entire lives. Not her birthdays or high school graduation or the trip to Nigeria.

And she couldn't remember the night of their first kiss, as sophomores after that track meet where he'd run over the competition. She couldn't remember his love for her. Then again, she never really understood his feelings for her, had she?

The nurse stepped away and Ruby's eyes followed her— until she started, her eyes wide on Abe.

24

His lips lifted in a grin. "Hi..."

"She can't remember. Not her name..."

He left the sentence as it was. The tips of his fingers searched for his back pockets—except he had put on jogging pants. He let his hands hang. "How are you feeling today?"

The corner of her lip lifted an inch. "I've been better."

He chuckled. *She might not remember, but she's still Ruby.* Abe stepped to the side of the bed. They had washed her hair. And brushed it. Clean, red strands draped across her shoulders.

"You came...before."

Her voice was raspy, like her mouth was dry. But he couldn't find a pitcher of water. Or a cup.

He met her eyes and his heart thrashed in his chest. So much he wanted to say, but... "I've come every day since you were admitted." *Forty-three days, including today.*

She gave a small nod, her eyes peering at him. "I remember your voice."

He took her hand and held it at his stomach, his fingers tracing the delicate skin around the medical tape. "I'm Abe. You and I were engaged."

Her cheeks turned a rosy pink. "We're engaged?"

"Umm, no. We were." *But she wouldn't know the difference, would she?* He released his breath, keeping her hand close to him. "The wedding was supposed to be in September, but it was broken off. Temporarily. So, you could find yourself."

Abe closed his eyes and let a groan bubble in his throat. *You just had to go and be honest, didn't you? Couldn't let it be for a second?*

Ruby giggled, her fingers tightening around his hand. "Isn't that ironic?" She rested back against the pillow, her face framed by healthy locks the color of autumn. "Now I'm trying to find myself again—for a different reason."

When she smiled, his breath caught. His Ruby—she was back.

Chapter 7

A nurse tucked a flimsy blanket around Ruby's hips. When she'd finished, Ruby settled the teddy bear against her side and replaced her clasped hands.

Abe had visited her every day during her hospital stay. He had been there during her transport to the rehab facility. He'd sat with her as she ate her dinner and shared with her about his first day as a software programmer, and how he surprised himself by being intrigued by the complexity of his new work.

He'd shared stories of Ruby and their relationship together. Most times she laughed so hard her stomach hurt and other times her head hurt trying to keep up with the details.

Today, he would come early with her parents to take her home. She could have walked out, but they had her sit in the wheelchair. And she didn't need the celebratory snack after breakfast, but she smiled and let the nurses love on her.

With a blanket around her jean-clad legs and holding a boo-boo bear—another unnecessary gift from one of the nurses—Ruby was wheeled out into the crisp air of early autumn.

The sun was bright and she had to squint and shield her eyes. Her parents rushed to kiss her on the cheek.

Ruby's lips inched higher. Abe was there, as he promised, holding the passenger car door. An expression of pure love and devotion.

"Hi, Ruby."

Her cheeks heated. "Hi, Abe."

He leaned over and kissed her cheek. Then held her shoulders as she stood up, took the step toward the door and slid inside.

The breath caught in her throat. On the dashboard were a dozen red roses, bound by a scarlet ribbon. Her hands trembled as Abe rested the bouquet in her lap. "As red as a ruby."

He kissed her again and helped himself into the back seat with her mother. Ruby wiped happy tears from her face.

Like a dream—but not. Words, a memory, she heard not long ago. Abe's voice. *"When you wake up, Ruby, I'll be here."*

She held the roses tight against the rapid beating of her heart. And he had kept his promise.

Ruby slid napkins into the holder, sticking several more when there was a gap. With her tongue between her lips, she went back into the kitchen to get the placemats—pretty ones with orange and yellow leaves—and a matching trivet the shape of a maple leaf for the center of the table.

The doorbell sounded and a squeal escaped her throat. She bounded back into the kitchen. "Pam? That's Abe. Is it okay if I...?"

"Yes, yes, dear." Her mother chuckled as she folded the towels. "Have fun."

She sprinted down the corridor of hardwood and cream-colored walls, sparse except for a painting of a lighthouse beaming in a stormy night. Yanking her purse to her shoulder, she thrust the door open. The breeze sailed through her hair she'd clipped to the side.

Abe smiled, his endearing brown eyes shining in the waning sun, and extended his elbow. She tucked her arm in his and they walked to his car, a reliable hand-me-down from

Ruby's dad, he'd told her.

As Abe opened the passenger car door, she asked, "What is Ruby's favorite color?"

He eyed her peach-colored sweater and washed-out jeans. "She didn't have one." He leaned an arm on the car door. As she slid into the passenger seat, the corner of his lips lifted. "Why do you ask?"

She lowered her eyes and fingered the hem of the sweater. "Her closet has a little bit of everything. Just wondering."

Giving her a small smile, he gently shut the door.

A second later, he joined her in the front seat and started the car. "Okay, the truth is, it's not she didn't have a favorite color, but she changed her mind so often." He reversed down the driveway. On the street, he shifted gears and started toward the restaurant. "Every week she claimed her favorite changed. Sometimes every hour."

"That makes sense." Ruby sat back and smiled, resting her hands in her lap. Her eyes drifted out the window to the reds of the trees on the side of the road. "The light shining in a prism was her favorite. Any color of the rainbow, depending on her mood."

He nodded, glancing at her. A smile in his eyes. A combination of shock and pleasure. "Yeah. That's right."

The conversation turned, him asking how her day was. When questioned himself, he kept his answer about work brief—and redirected the focus back to her, asking how she was feeling. He was so thoughtful and considerate, it warmed her heart. Such a caring man who loved her deeply. *Why would I break up with such a kind-hearted soul?*

When they reached the restaurant, he took her arm again and didn't release his hold until they were seated at a table in the back.

"This is our favorite place. The food's great, the music isn't too loud, and the service is decent." He grinned, sliding into the seat across from her.

"And the ambience is lovely," she added, taking the

moment to look at the brass lantern hanging above their table.

He watched her, one eyebrow perched. "It's nice ambience. Actually."

She laughed, lifting a menu. "Sorry. Did I say something?"

He shook his head, opening a menu.

She narrowed her eyes. "Abe, *what* did I say? Was it something—"

"It's nothing." He flashed her a smile and then bent his head over the menu.

They spent the next few minutes reading in silence.

"Oh!" She closed her menu and leaned over the table. "Has Ruby—I mean, have *I* ever split a dish with you? Like I share mine with you and vice versa?"

"No, but I'm sure *she* would have if *she'd* thought of it." His eyes danced as he leaned in. "Truth is, we didn't come here much. More Panera Bread kind of dates. Up until recently I was in college, so we reserved this place for special occasions."

He waggled his eyebrows and she laughed.

"Sharing sounds like a fun idea. What are you getting?" he said.

"Baked ziti. How about you?"

The side of his mouth fell. He sagged back in his seat and spent considerable time unfolding the cloth napkin.

She crossed her forearms on the table and peered at him. "Abe, what is it?"

"Sorry." He clenched the napkin in his fist and faced her. "I'm lactose-intolerant."

"I'm so sorry. I didn't know." Snapping open the menu, she gleaned the choices.

"You couldn't have known. Order what you want, it's completely okay." But the way he kept his eyes lowered, taking up the napkin to fold it in half next to his plate, made her think this wasn't okay.

Her eyes on the menu options, she wet her lips. "What would Ruby order?"

He looked at her from under his eyebrows, his lip tipping into a smile. "Speaking in third person again?"

Her chest tightened and her vision swam. She pressed her lips together before her emotions crumpled.

"Sorry. I shouldn't have said that." He shrugged. "She would get the baked ziti. Why not? Oh, and…" He flipped his menu over to see the list of beverages. "There's a non-alcoholic drink section. Smoothies, virgin cocktails, flavored waters. She'd go for that too. Especially something like strawberry lemonade. Too sour for me, but she liked to try new things."

He lifted his face and managed a smile. But his cheeks were blanched, the light had faded from his eyes.

She snapped the menu closed. "I'm getting spaghetti and meatballs. End of discussion."

Abe cocked his head, peering at her. "Spaghetti? Really?"

Heat drifted up her neck. She took a sip of ice water. "Yes, absolutely."

He rested an elbow on the table and smoothed his jaw. "I'm getting the salmon and baked potato. You should totally go for the steak."

She wrinkled her nose. "Red meat is a bit heavy. Even Pam's meatloaf yesterday was a little too much." Setting the glass down, she met his eyes.

"You call your mom 'Pam'?" His voice softened. "Not comfortable yet?"

She bit back on her lower lip.

"Someday you'll remember everything." But his voice didn't hold conviction. And when she met his gaze, he looked away.

Chapter 8

Abe tightened his grip on the steering wheel. Ruby had gotten more and more quiet during their evenings together, but this afternoon after church she hadn't said three words.

He got it. Really, he did. There were a lot of people who saw her today and couldn't understand. Some stayed away and others were too generous with their sympathy. He felt the awkwardness, the hurt.

But that didn't give her license to hide from him. When she'd asked to go straight home, he hadn't argued. But now? It was as if she had slept through the entire service, as if she hadn't listened to the sermon.

He made a third attempt at conversation. "Mind if I tell you what struck me?"

She shrugged. Maybe. He couldn't be certain with his eyes on the road.

He spoke freely on the idea of *maybe*. "The part where the pastor said, 'The righteous died for the unrighteous, so even the most unrighteous could obtain God's full righteousness.' I think I paraphrased all wrong, but that really got to me. Just never thought of the depth of Jesus' grace before."

He stole a glance at her, for all the good it did. She was looking out the window. He released a sigh. "What's eating at you?"

"I just want to go home." Her voice was small. In his

twenty-some years of knowing her, he'd never known her to be eager to get home.

He drove up her driveway and cut the engine. "Please, Ruby, tell me."

"Stop calling me that!" She fled from the car and across the lawn. He caught up to her when she fumbled with the key in the lock.

"Sorry, okay? I just… What should I call you?"

"I don't know." Frustrated, she threw the keys at the door. "I don't know!" She thrust her palm against the wood. One, two, three times.

Abe winced when she leaned against the frame and shook out her tingling palm. "I'm sick of the awkwardness. Of the look of surprise on everyone's face."

"It's only a matter of time before your memory returns."

She nailed him a look that shook his insides. "What am I supposed to do in the meantime? I look like Ruby, but I'm an empty shell."

When she retrieved the keys and tried the lock again he took her shoulders. "I know it's awkward now, but we're partially to blame. You're Ruby, but we shouldn't assume—"

"Call me Olivia." The key slid into the lock.

"Why?"

She turned to face him. "It's Ruby's middle name."

"I know that, but why?"

"So that when I act like I've never seen someone dice onions before, or suddenly have a fascination over a car model—"

"Oh, yeah. That." He chuckled. "When you've seen your dad build the same car model for twenty years, you'll get sick of—"

"Or when I can't remember my best friend's food allergy, I won't feel like such an idiot." She let herself in and the lock clicked shut.

Olivia flipped through the thin pages of the Bible. *Ruby's* Bible. Every other sentence was underlined. There was some color-coding going on, but Olivia couldn't make sense of it.

She located the third chapter of Romans and re-read the passage from the church service.

"But now the righteousness of God has been manifested apart from the law..."

The phrase "righteousness of God" had been underlined three times. Her stomach turned to gravel and she closed the Bible, shutting it in the drawer of the nightstand.

She lay back on the navy-blue and plum comforter and looked at the canary-yellow walls. For a girl who couldn't decide on a favorite color, she sure used a lot of them.

The phone in her purse dinged. When she saw the new text, her cheeks warmed.

Abe: Hi, Olivia :)

He had used her new name. It had been a dumb idea, but she was frustrated and desperate. And didn't she have a point? When people called her "Ruby," even if they were careful and considerate, more often than not she misinterpreted something they referred to. And ultimately scared people. Like they were looking at a ghost.

Which wasn't far from the truth.

When she told Pam to call her by her middle name, the woman started blubbering about missing Ruby. Gosh, she sounded like her daughter had died the day of the car accident. And maybe she had. Until Olivia could remember, Ruby was no more.

The words she had said to Abe were honest. People saw Ruby but inside was hollow. Empty. Nothing existed. Her mind, her heart, her soul wasn't there.

Her soul.

Her phone dinged.

Abe: I'm sorry I hurt your feelings today.

And Olivia realized she hadn't acknowledged his first text. He probably thought she was still bitter. But she wasn't. She already missed him.

Her fingers flew over the letters.

Olivia: I forgive you. And I'm sorry too. Friends?
Abe: Thanks :)
Abe: But I'd like us to be more than friends.

Olivia grinned and waited. A full minute later:

Abe: Are you free tonight?

Olivia pulled her knees to her chest and watched the screen until it went dark from inactivity. She sighed and lifted the phone.

Olivia: Free for what?

She could imagine his head fall back. His guttural groan. *Yes, Abe, you have to ask. No short cuts.*

Even if, as Abe had told her, Ruby had been his first girlfriend. That he'd never had to woo her because they'd always hung out together and their relationship had evolved naturally.

If Olivia really was a new neighbor, if Ruby really had died and Abe had to start over—

Abe: Olivia, will you go out with me?

Lame. But he got credit for trying. Nibbling on her bottom lip, she responded.

Olivia: I have to ask my mom.

She grinned and waited a beat.

> Olivia: Kidding! When and where?
> Abe: You got me :)
> Abe: Tonight? 7pm? I'll pick you up.
> Olivia: Okay.
> Abe: Love you!

Olivia's fingers hovered over the screen. She wanted to say something snarky about how they haven't dated yet and he couldn't possibly be in love with her.

But the sentiment settled in her gut and warmed her insides. He was kind and gentle, patient and understanding. Someone she could love back.

In the end, she decided to not text back at all, but instead hustled to her closet to decide what to wear for tonight's date with Abe.

Chapter 9

Abe got into his car and drove it to the next driveway. Slammed it in park. *This is ridiculous.*

But if he wanted a chance with Ruby—er, Olivia—losing a little pride wouldn't hurt. Soon, they'd be in a relationship. He'd invite her over like always. They'd play board games and tease each other non-stop.

Because he knew Ruby was in there. Now and again he'd see pieces of her in the phrases Olivia would use and her expressions. Her desire for adventure, to learn something new, to not settle.

To never settle.

That was her most profound trait. And the number one reason he loved her.

Olivia. Or Ruby.

This is ridiculous.

He made his way up the driveway. What's in a name anyway? Sure, he could have been more considerate but wasn't he trying?

And that text *"I have to ask my mom"* irked him to no end. Does she *have* to be difficult?

He rang the doorbell and adjusted the daisies in his hand. But Ruby was alive and giving him a chance. That meant something.

Pam opened the door.

She rolled her eyes and looked over her shoulder, as annoyed as he was with this game, and then leaned against the doorframe. "How can I help you, Abe?"

Frowning, he regarded her with an arched eyebrow. Olivia was coaching her mom? Heat drifted up his neck. What was next? An interview with her dad?

He cleared his throat. "I've come to ask your daughter, Olivia, out on date."

Her lips hitched up. "I'll go get *Olivia.* Come on in."

Abe sighed and stepped into the living room, taking a seat at the familiar blue-and-beige patchwork sofa. The television screen was cockeyed, as it had been since they installed it three years ago.

His gaze drifted up and a smirk passed his lips. Still hanging on the wall after all these years was Ruby's watercolor rendition from youth group of the new Jerusalem coming from heaven. It had been Ruby's idea to smear glue over the whole thing to make the city walls shine.

He heard footsteps on the staircase and shot to his feet, the daisies held in both hands.

This won't be so bad. I'll introduce myself, she'll tell me some stuff, and we'll settle in real quick.

Olivia stepped into the room. Her hair was pinned up again in a stupid barrette. And she was wearing a yellowish-orange jumper even Ruby wouldn't wear.

He recollected as best he could. *This isn't Ruby. She wouldn't know her preferences.*

So, maybe this game had a purpose after all. "Hi, Olivia." He extended the flowers. "These are for you."

"Thank you. They're lovely." Her eyes lit up and her lips lifted. Exuberantly happy. Except Ruby had never been *exuberantly happy.*

His stomach sank. What if Ruby really was gone? What if he'd truly lost her? He extended his elbow and she wound her arm in his. Would he ever be able to love this imitation?

37

Abe had tried. He really had. But by the end of the evening, he was ready to go home. She could sense it too. Whatever glimpses of Ruby he'd seen before, he couldn't find them tonight. Why would he? She was Olivia.

And who was Olivia anyway? What was he supposed to ask? He knew more than she did!

Coming into the foyer of his home, he tossed his jacket at the hook and missed. It slumped to the floor. Not caring, he flopped on the couch and covered his face with his arm.

"How'd it go?" The sound of a kitchen towel being whipped over his mother's shoulder. She always had a towel over her shoulder when she was cleaning the kitchen. One of her quirks.

What if he had to notice it for the first time? To appreciate rather than to take little things for granted?

And how would his mother respond if he paid attention?

Abe sat up, resting his forearms on his knees and letting his head hang. "She's not Ruby."

"No, she's not." His mother padded over in her slippers and bathrobe and sat beside him. "You dated Olivia today, honey."

He turned to look at her, an eyebrow cocked. "You do realize we're talking about the same person?"

"Maybe that's your problem." She rested a hand on his back. The comfort of a mother who loved him through and through, no matter what he did, who he decided to become.

And that was just it. Abe loved Ruby no matter what she decided to call herself. Or what she decided to wear—as long as she kept that strange dress she wore today in her closet.

"It's time to stop searching for Ruby and start loving Olivia."

"Easier said than done."

She rubbed his back a final time before heading back to the kitchen. "If you don't, you'll lose both of them."

38

After work on Monday, he decided he'd walk over to get Olivia and they'd come back to get his car. No more driving next door.

Sure, it wasn't fair. But if she was a new neighbor, wouldn't she understand? Completely reasonable request. Heck, he'd even worn his good shoes. And he'd never done that with Ruby, not even on anniversaries.

He knocked on the door with another bouquet of flowers. This time a variety of orange and red, an autumn arrangement. Something different. He couldn't bring himself to carry over a jar of olives. Not yet.

Every now and again he wanted to turn to her, look her deep in the eyes and ask her to call him Paul. But then he reconsidered, thinking the joke might not go down too well. Too early for teasing. Would there ever be a good time to joke about her amnesia?

Olivia opened the door—and Abe's heart stopped. Wrapped around her neck was an indigo shawl.

He staggered back. "Are you doing that *on purpose?*"

Her eyebrows lifted. "What?"

"It's not funny, Ru—whoever you are!" He sidestepped to the porch swing and cradled his head in his hands.

Leaving for Nigeria. The reason she left. *"I want to date other guys."*

This isn't Olivia's fault.

He wiped his eyes. Had he been crying?

Somewhere in that time, he'd dropped the flowers. He stood up and came back to the door, scooping the crushed bouquet off the concrete step. Olivia still stood there, her jaw unhinged, her eyes unblinking.

Still wearing the shawl.

He swallowed and when he opened his mouth, a sound like a sob came out instead. "Could you take the shawl off? Sorry."

He turned and sat on the porch steps.

What a creep he was. He couldn't have explained? Couldn't have told her earlier?

Being with Olivia when she looked, sounded and *dressed* like Ruby was hard. Really hard.

Olivia sat beside him. The color in her outfit was gone. All she wore now was a white cotton dress. *And she's probably freezing, you idiot.*

"Sorry," he muttered.

She scooted closer to him and slid an arm through the crook of his elbow. "Tell me about her."

Chapter 10

The frozen landscape in front of Abe morphed into burnt oranges and magenta-reds. Pine trees with a fresh coat of snow dotted the periphery of the hilly park district.

Other than the group of geese that squawked on a pond and flew away, all was quiet and still. As if heaven held this moment as sacred, the finale of the Lord's Day, in glorious majesty.

Abe exhaled and his breath swirled into a dense fog one instant and then was gone.

The first day of the week had been Ruby's busiest. No way would she be caught sitting around, doing nothing. After church, teenagers needed to eat. And then they needed love and prayer and comfort before heading back to another week of school and upcoming finals.

Always an upcoming-something. If not finals, then the Christmas program, or Easter service.

Even before Ruby joined the youth ministry she had always been moving, always changing her mind and trying a new thing. How many times had he watched Ruby dash from one activity to the next? As if she needed to juggle three service opportunities, so she would never be left with a void in her schedule. Heaven forbid Ruby ever *stopped*.

Olivia cuddled deeper into Abe's side and he tightened his hold around her. "Cold?"

She shook her head against his shoulder, padded by his winter coat. "I love this."

"Me too."

He released a long, steamy breath. "Ruby would never have been able to sit long enough to love this."

"Hmm."

The thought pricked at his heart. That wasn't fair, was it? For all the times he'd *wanted* to, he'd never sat Ruby down and tried to convince her to pause her schedule for a moment. Not once had he initiated the idea they do something as ridiculous as *be together.*

Instead, he'd waited for her. He waited until her whirlwind of activity slowed, until he had her attention long enough to tell her how much she meant to him, to kiss her with all the bottled-up emotion he kept for that right moment.

But the time had never come.

As if on cue, Olivia pulled away to look at him, a smile slowly spreading across her face, lighting her eyes.

His heart pitter-pattered. *That time is now.*

Now?

The woman looking at him, who was lost, but also found. Peaceful, but haunted. Lovely, but knowing her face represented someone else.

This sweet version who could sit for thirty minutes and do absolutely nothing but enjoy the view. Who craved this time— not because she couldn't remember, but because she bathed in the new sensations. Every one of them. Soaked up the colors of the sunset, the smells of pine, the feel of frost. Even lapping up the attention he gave her. Every second became a gift to be cherished.

But to tell her? Wasn't this too soon? Too impulsive?

Her gaze softened and the air filled his lungs, enlarging his chest, the fog misting in front of his face.

Because, yeah, his heart had shifted lately, ever since Olivia let him open up about everything he missed about Ruby, everything that reminded him of her.

She listened to him and took pains to be considerate of his need to grieve. He hadn't seen the indigo scarf again—or anything else Ruby had worn for that matter.

Olivia had managed to convince her parents to buy a full closet of clothes, from flattering dresses to new sneakers. And recently a new coat and boots. All of Ruby's clothes were packed in bins and stored under her bed.

And she hadn't stopped there.

He missed the coconut scent, but when Olivia had tossed the scented lip balms and switched out her shampoos it was like he could breathe.

Even today to endure hot water mixed with cocoa rather than drink the creamier hot chocolate—it meant a lot to him. Gave him some confidence he hadn't had before. Convinced him he mattered, that his dreams were worth pursuing.

And that was only the beginning. He started to notice *her* in a whole new light too. The softer materials and pastel hues accentuated the calmness about her. As wonderful and as beautiful as ever—but deeper, richer, more poignant. As if when she awoke, she embraced life fully this time around, holding nothing back.

His veins pulsated. Even though an icy wind bit at his cheeks, his face heated. "I'm glad you're enjoying yourself."

The brown hues in her hazel eyes glowed in the fading light of the sunset, her fragrance-free lips shimmered.

More than glad. The idea delighted him.

Tell her. Now.

Warmth swirled in his chest and he threaded his gloved fingers within hers. "Olivia?"

He could kiss her now. He could—but he couldn't. He didn't have the nerve. Even if his pulse raced at the thought of her in his arms, of being beside her. And now, to just sit and be. Something he had always wanted to do with Ruby but never had.

Which was the reason he couldn't draw the look-alike close, to brush his lips against hers. Who would he be kissing?

And what would it mean?

A shiver ran up his spine. What was he thinking? Wasn't he doing all this, the dates, the watching and waiting, reminding her and keeping patient, so she *would* remember? So Ruby would come back to him? He swore he would never leave her.

A chill coursed his body, settling into his bones.

The light shone in Olivia's eyes and with it, a rosy-cheeked smile. "What is it, Abe?"

The words stuck in his throat.

Was Ruby merely buried inside, not able to remember— or was the woman in front of him only Olivia? The woman who appreciated spending a lazy day together, who could simply live in the moment. Who was content to be loved by him.

Wait. *Love?*

Looking at her, being as close as he was, he had the zaniest idea to taste that lip gloss, to test that notion.

But...not yet. Because he couldn't be in love with Olivia—could he?

Regardless, he needed to determine if Ruby was in there somewhere, if the woman who lived next door still lingered. Unless she was gone for good.

He snagged the two empty thermoses and extended his hand. "Would you do me a favor?"

"What is it?"

When she took his hand and stood, he squeezed her fingers. *There is just enough time left in the day.* His heart sped to a staccato. *And the rink is open until late.*

He quirked a smile at her as they started back to the club house. "Something different."

Abe gave the laces on Olivia's skate an extra hard tug, then straightened. Her curls fell across her shoulder as she peered at him. "The *entire* time? No kidding around and letting me go all of sudden?"

"I won't let go of you for one second. Honest."

Her lavender leggings wrinkled at the knee as she rotated her ankle, her eyes on the gleam of the blade. "Has Ruby skated?"

His head felt weightless, the tips of his fingers tingled. He drew out an easy smile. "Never."

And Ruby has never spent an afternoon walking around a pond. Or drinking hot chocolate on a bench in sub-freezing temps.

He led Olivia to the opening onto the ice. Only a dozen other souls braved the cold today. A perfect day for a skate.

She planted herself at the doorway with both hands clutching the railing. He stepped on the ice and pivoted to face Olivia, so close to her his skate bumped the step. His heart beat triple time, maybe as fast-paced as hers—except he wasn't afraid of a broken ankle. He couldn't wait to see her reaction. To see what Olivia was made of.

Olivia was staring at the ice, her lips pursed. No Ruby in sight. Just a girl afraid of trying something new.

With one hand around her back, he unlatched her gloved fingers from the railing with the other. "Easy does it."

She stepped down to an unstable wobble on nothing but metal and grabbed at his arm. "Oh, this is awful."

"You're doing great."

She placed her other foot solid, the pressure increasing around his forearm.

And all the while, Abe felt the breath leave and enter his lungs, his heart making demands on his rib cage.

Had it been Ruby's habit to rush? Or had the busyness been a way to bury her fears?

Not that it mattered now. Ruby wasn't here.

Olivia was looking out at the other skaters weaving around the rink. A group whizzed in front of them, the swish of blades on ice, amused laughter swelling and receding as they past.

Abe drew in a breath and released it slowly. "Doing okay?"

"This is going to take forever to learn."

"Not forever." He licked his lips. Despite the cold, heat swirled across his torso, radiating down his arms. And something broke free from his chest.

Ruby isn't here.

Abe gnawed on the side of his cheek, keenly aware of his arm around her, how her coat grazed his.

Using slow strides, he started around the periphery of the rink. "How's that?"

She pressed her lips together, something like a snort coming from her throat.

He stifled a chuckle.

As he skated backwards with her in his arms he admired the crosshatch at the bridge of her nose, the tender flesh of her lip caught between her teeth.

He let them come to a gradual stop near the wall. "Okay." He exhaled a breath, the steam misting between them. "Your turn. Start with your left leg."

Her back stiffened under his hand, her arms tensed.

An image of his former fiancée flickered in his mind. Except instead of an ice skating rink, it had been an open dance floor. When prompted by him, she turned on her heel and left the reception. Nothing he said could convince her to give a slow dance a try. Ruby had refused to give it a second thought.

His stomach clamped. *Ruby never trusted me.* His throat stung. He blinked hot moisture from his eyes. *All those years... But you ran away so fast. If you would have stayed, you would have known...*

Fresh breath filled his lungs, the ache in his chest released. Olivia was still on the ice.

Even though trying something new was terrifying, Olivia trusted Abe enough to stay. She was giving him a chance.

And Abe wanted to take a chance too.

Exchanging his hands, he slid next to her side. "See that

advertisement on the wall?"

Her eyes flickered to the poster six feet away. She didn't nod, didn't move a muscle. Didn't even breathe.

But she wasn't bailing. Wasn't twisting in his arms, looking to escape before she did something as embarrassing as fail at something she had yet to try.

She put her security in his hands—literally. That he wouldn't let her fall. That she was safe with him. Whether that was true or not was a different matter. Because she *could* fall. He couldn't promise she wouldn't.

What if they failed? What if they fell in a heap on the rock-hard ice? What then?

His eyes trailed to Olivia, who quivered under his grip. He trembled at the responsibility, the uncertainty. What would it look like for Olivia to let go of abandon, to fly on her own?

If she was willing to take the risk to stay on the ice, then he would too.

He cleared his throat. "When we reach that poster, you say stop and we'll stop, okay?"

Her nod was short, as stiff as fresh leather. The steam misted as she breathed through her nose. In—then a whoosh out. In, and then...

But before he could tell her to relax, she pushed off with her left foot. He stayed with her and a second later, she moved her right foot.

His hand firm on hers, he let his face break into a smile. "Olivia, are you seeing this?"

Her eyes glued on the ice in front of her. The ad came and went. But something told him she *did* see. She was very much aware.

And with that thought, he stamped out the remnants of doubt. In its place, a confidence pulled his chest muscles tighter, strengthening his core.

"You're leaning a bit. Try to straighten your back."

But as she rounded her shoulders, her feet forgot to move and she wobbled. He chuckled, keeping her steady.

Her lips drooped. "Sorry, it's so much…"

"You're doing great."

She glanced at him with the briefest of smiles and pink on her cheeks. His chest hummed. No longer for the past he regretted, but for the future he hoped for. Dreamed of. Aspired to.

Because this was what he lived for. The joy of a mile-marker being overcome. Of seeing a child blow out candles, being hugged by family and friends, to capture a moment of time when a new stage of life is celebrated.

And to see the most significant person in his life seize this reality for herself—it took his breath from his lungs.

He steered her left as they came to the curved part of the wall. And as their route straightened again, her shoulders hunched forward, her chin tucked against the soft material of her scarf.

He squeezed her fingers, softening his tone. "It'll be easier to keep your balance if your back is straight. Lift your chin, honey. Eyes forward."

Ever so slowly, she inched her chin higher until she was looking straight ahead.

"There you go." Heat crawled up his neck, spilling onto his face. *This is Olivia.*

Pride filled him. Clamped on him so tight he could hardly take a breath, his smile so wide it hurt his face.

"Chin up, Olivia. You're doing it. You're skating."

The profile of her face broke into a smile. Then a soft laughter dribbled from her mouth. "Oh my gosh, I'm skating. *I'm skating!*"

The pace was slow, she had his hand in a death grip, but her knees had relaxed. Her momentum drove her forward, experiencing a victory—while doing absolutely nothing of significance. No award. No applause. Not breaking anyone's record except her own.

Simply the accomplishment of claiming life, looking inside and discovering herself.

A revelation she wouldn't have experienced if she hadn't taken Abe's hand, if she hadn't relinquished control for those few seconds. A moment when trust gave way to something new.

With her eyes bright and her smile stretched, Abe tugged her a distance from the wall and braked gradually, keeping Olivia at arms-length.

Her hand firm in his, he started to slide his other hand from the small of her back.

Her head shot up, her eyes wild and bugged. "You promised you wouldn't let go."

His heart squeezed. He wouldn't let go—ever. He couldn't wash away his grin. "Just getting a better grip on you."

She cocked her head, the corners of her lips tipping up. "Are you going to twirl me?"

He ground his skates in the ice, trying to anchor his legs as bubbles of pleasure sizzled and popped through him. "That's the hope."

He took her wrist and turned her in place, slowly once... Twice.

And her nervous giggle dissolved into a squeal of delight. Her flaming locks draped across her back in their natural waves—not straightened as Ruby had styled her hair. Hot pink earmuffs and a matching scarf knotted at the collar of her cream-colored coat replaced Ruby's black knit hat and coat.

Placing a hand on her arm, he slowed her rotation until she was again facing him. The color of her cheeks had deepened, her parted lips exhaled wisps of vapor, as breathless as he was.

He pulled her to him, his gaze held by the smile that lifted the corner of her lips. Soft lips, looking delicious.

The final crimp in his heart smoothed to silk. Because being strapped in a seat wouldn't have fixed her to the ground—it was the only way to achieve lift off, to get out of the earth's atmosphere, to travel to the moon and beyond. Trust was the launching pad to take off to greater heights she never would have accomplished on her own.

As he took her hands and pulled her back to their track near the wall, Olivia laughed and he joined in. A belly laugh, rich and free. Because, as much as he loved her, as much as he missed her, Ruby was gone. And perhaps it would be best if Ruby never returned.

Chapter 11

Oliva bent her head over the Bible, pressing her fingers down into the crease to read the verse again. *"However, to the one who does not work but trusts God who justifies the ungodly, their faith is credited as righteousness."*

The words warmed her heart, smeared her with confidence. Taking up her pen, she wrote her answer in the space provided, but the phrase, *"trusts God"* went deeper than ink on paper. This was *her* verse along with the dozens like it she'd read, heard, and meditated on in the Book of Romans these past few weeks.

She glanced up—and the air got trapped in her throat. Abe was staring at her, a whimsical smile on his lips. Not the first time she caught him staring, but ever since ice skating on Sunday, a smile lit up his face more often. And maybe the same had happened to her. She had a fun time and would do it again. Or something else new and zany, broken ankles notwithstanding.

She lifted her eyebrows. "What's up?"

He cocked his head toward the page in front of him. "Did you look up the definition for credit yet?"

She shook her head, glancing at the sheet. Abe was one question ahead of her.

"Be right back." He winked at her and her cheeks warmed as he went to the bookcase for the dictionary.

The smell of chocolate drifted into the living room, followed by the oven door snapping shut.

Abe plopped on the floor at their makeshift study at the coffee table, the heavy book opened. "Oh, credit is from the Latin *creditum,* meaning a balance in a person's favor." He turned the book toward her, taking up his pen. "It's also a version of *credere,* which means believe."

He wrote the answer, his opposite arm resting on the table. Today he wore a brick-red sweater she'd seen before. Perhaps the material was soft. Or perhaps red was his favorite color. In either case, the sweater made his brown hair and eyes a shade darker. And ten times more handsome.

Heat crawled up her neck. She bent her head to read the next question on the lesson paper. *In your own words, how would you explain...?*

Jeanette Coleman stepped out of the kitchen, several bulging grocery bags hanging from her shoulder. "The brownies are done, so help yourself. I'm just dropping this off at the Salvation Army and will be back in about an hour."

Abe met her at the door, planting a kiss on the cheek. "Be safe, Mom. Love you."

Olivia jerked her head down, nibbling on her lip. A thought nipped at her... But she had been hoping, waiting, praying.

"Time for a sugar break?" Abe came to stand in front of her, his hand extended. She slid her fingers into his palm, the shock of heat as his fingers curled around her hand and sent goosebumps up her arms. Only the slightest tug as he helped her up, as if he didn't want to hurt her. As if she were precious and wanted and cherished.

But that wasn't true. She was a stranger, a foreigner. Only a temporary placeholder until the true girlfriend returned.

Olivia perched on a stool in the kitchen as Abe cut into the brownies. Steam drifted from where the knife was inserted and Olivia breathed in deep, letting the fudgey-richness fill her nostrils. "Mmm, smells delicious."

He met her eye and the corner of his lips tipped up. "I *know* you remember the smell of brownies."

She shrugged, letting her lips curl into a shy smile.

Abe served two plates, sinking the fork into his piece. "Tomorrow I'll be helping with a late party. But I'm only a second host, so I don't have to get there until four." His lips closed around the bite of brownie. "The drawback is I'll probably be late coming home. Big parties tend to leave a big mess."

She stuck the tines of her fork in the dessert.

"Could you come near the end, so I could show you around the party rooms? I'll save you a balloon." He waggled his eyebrows. "If we had balloons that is."

She laughed. "I'd love to. Has Ruby ever—"

The words jammed in her throat, her cheeks heating. She didn't know why she kept bringing her up. Like an old girlfriend. Or a deceased spouse.

No, that wasn't true. She knew *exactly* why she inserted Ruby everywhere. She didn't want Abe to forget. And she didn't want to forget her place.

But if anyone asked about her curiosity, she'd say she wanted to ready herself for people's strange looks. Because if Ruby *had* visited the park district multiple times, people would recognize her, right? And looking lost would be suspicious, wouldn't it?

But knowing the territory and history hadn't helped her when she was ecstatically greeted at church by people she couldn't name.

"She didn't come often." Abe cut his brownie into halves. Then cut it again into quarters. He lifted a shoulder and let it drop.

She gnawed at the corner of her lip. *Of course,* Ruby had been to the Schaumburg Park District if Abe had been working there since high school.

Her stomach turned and she rested her fork on the plate. All this would be better if only God would grant her request.

If only Ruby would wake up.

Finishing his final quarter, Abe hopped up to fill a glass with water. From the sink he gave her that smile where one side lifted higher than the other. "But I think *you* would like to see the party rooms."

"I'll tell Tom to drop me off." She lifted her fork. But she had no intention to eat. Because along with his sweet voice came his promise filled with hope and prayer for his beloved. *"When you wake up, Ruby, I'll be here."*

And no one wanted Ruby to wake up more than Olivia did.

She sighed and sank her fork sideways down the brownie to scrape off a slice.

"It's reasonable you can't drive yet." Abe took a quick sip and set the glass on the counter. "I wouldn't want you to."

If only that was all it is.

She lifted a shoulder, a smile drifting to her lips, even as her gaze darted away—and landed on the framed portrait above the sink. A boy with dark hair, probably Abe in his youth, stood next to Jeanette. And a man stood behind Abe, both hands planted on Abe's shoulders.

She swallowed around the sticky mass in her throat and took a deep breath until the smell of chocolate and the citrus multi-purpose cleaner his mom used in the kitchen eased the ache in her heart.

"Why don't you ask?" His arms still across his chest, but his eyes were soft. Curious.

Abe's voice was full of compassion and genuine sympathy. Except it was *his* father who had died and it was *he* who had to recount the tragedy—to the very person who had been at his side the whole time. Whose family had undoubtedly helped him through.

She drew in her breath. "Because you shouldn't have to tell me."

His lips tucked. "Why not?"

"Because…" Words jumbled in her mind, but nothing came to her tongue. Nothing coherent. There were too many reasons—didn't he know that?

And when Ruby returned—because she would—Abe would realize he'd entered into this pain for a second time for nothing.

The back of her eyes stung. *Ruby, please, wake up.*

"He was diagnosed with pancreatic cancer when I was ten and died two months later."

Olivia jerked her head up. "Abe, you don't have to—"

"I want to."

Chapter 12

Olivia clenched her fingers in her lap, a band wrapping around her chest and pulling tight.

In long strides, Abe crossed the kitchen to take his plate and help himself to another brownie. "I was mostly confused. One day Dad and I were playing catch outside and a week later he was bed-ridden." Abe cut off a piece and stuck it in his mouth. "All of sudden I was the only male in the house. My mom was strong, but she was hurting. It all happened so fast."

He pierced the brownie with his fork but didn't bring the sliver to his mouth. "Your mom was always around, cooking, laundry, whatever. We needed help paying medical bills, making calls to the insurance company, stuff like that."

Olivia pictured a little boy who suddenly lost his father, the closest male influence in his life.

And Ruby? Where was she? Beside her mother, sorting socks? Or was she beside Abe, holding his hand and bringing him trinkets from a dollar store to cheer him up?

Olivia would never know. Because she wasn't going to ask.

Abe wiped his lips on a napkin. "But your dad helped me the most. He met with me every day." His eyes met Olivia's and gave her a smile. "He would sit me down here and listen. A whole bunch of listening. Not just about death and heaven, but about schoolwork and paper planes."

"Paper planes?"

Abe's lips lifted higher and he nodded. "Your dad makes gigantic paper planes with butcher paper. He made one that flew fifty feet. Awesome."

She bit back on her lip. Something else Ruby would have known.

"But the real work was when your dad left at night. He said he would pray for me when he got home. And I felt that, you know? The nudging. That I lost my dad, but there was Someone who I needed to meet."

"Your Heavenly Father?"

His smile shrank. A faraway look came to his eyes, which were now glistening in the recessed lights of his family's kitchen. Remembering those conversations from twelve years ago? Or did he realize he was telling his story to the girl who had been there? Who shouldn't be surprised at the details?

"The conversations turned, I don't know when, but we started talking over the Bible a lot more. And not a day would go by when I wouldn't learn something about my Everlasting Father, who would never die, never go away. When Jesus was abandoned so I could be adopted…" Abe grabbed a napkin and dabbed his eyes. "Forsaken, so I could have the same position and intimacy Jesus had with the Father. And that's what I have. That's what my dad blessed me with."

Tears leaked from her eyes and she cupped her mouth. Her heart stirred at the emotion she saw in his face, the confidence she heard his voice.

She closed her mouth just in time before she voiced her thoughts. *Did Ruby find the same clarity when she was baptized six years later?*

"Happy tears. Honest." He crumpled the napkin and smiled at her. But his eyes were still wet. "I've been so blessed, first to have known my dad as long as I did, and now to know my Father with a capital F, who guides me today and always will. Including yours, that makes three fathers who have loved me and carried me until now. This is the most blessed life, Olivia. But that's my biased opinion." His eyes twinkled, all but a light sheen remained. Peace radiated from the smile that tugged at his lips.

And her heart crumpled like the napkin he had discarded.

She had assumed his testimony would overwhelm him, would bring him to that dark place and wound him anew. But she never expected the effect would happen to her. She bit her lip as her chin began to tremble.

"Olivia."

She turned in her seat, so her back was toward him and covered her face when the tears started to spill.

"Sweetheart." His hands were light on her shoulders. "I *wanted* to tell you."

She shook her head, her throat thick with emotion.

Even if she could find her voice, she wouldn't be able to utter the prayer of her soul out loud. How could she begin to explain the loneliness in her heart, the despair that hovered over her like a shadow? That her yearning for peace was compounded by the torture of not being known at church? Even if she couldn't remember her past, the confidence Abe spoke of scorched her soul with possibility. Abe's identity, his assurance of who he was—Olivia wanted that.

She couldn't endure another Sunday of Abe having to explain her amnesia following the accident to as many church members as they encountered. To have another visitor fling her arms around Olivia, while she was frozen with fear.

But was transferring churches the answer? Or would she have the same challenges at a different location? *Lord God, what about me? Can I have such certainty of who I am?*

Olivia adjusted the clip in her hair, snapping it back in place. "We should get back to the Bible lesson."

Abe stepped in front of her, preventing her from leaving the stool. He touched her chin, lifting her face until she was looking at him. "That last part, about Jesus on the cross, I just thought of that in the instant when I was telling you. I hadn't connected it before."

His gaze circled her face, coming to land on her eyes. Holding there with sockets of flame. "Happy tears, Olivia. I don't think it was coincidence you were here when it happened."

She pressed her lips closed, holding the breath in her lungs.

"There are things Ruby knows that you don't and I'm starting to see that. Sure, you need to be reminded of some stuff—but there are a hundred *new* things I'm discovering now that I want to share with you."

"Except that…" Heat collected in the back of her eyes. She was trembling now, a knot forming at the base of her gut. *I don't belong here.*

"She's gone." The creases buried deeper in the corners of his eyes, his lips pulled in. "All I see is Olivia."

She forced her voice through the congestion and thickness in her throat. "Don't give up. Don't you dare!"

His fingertips slid along her jawline to cradle her cheek, leaving a trail of fire in its wake. "I wanted to tell you about my dad for a long time. Trust me, there was joy in telling you."

Abe pressed closer until she was certain he could feel her heart thrash against her ribs. Or was she feeling his?

"But there is one other thing I need to tell you." He cradled her face in his hands. Kissed her forehead. Trailing his pecks down her cheek, his fingers feather-light against her face. He found her lips. Delicate, as if he didn't want to break her. Gradual, as if to not scare her.

Her body vibrated at his touch, her spine turned to jelly and only his gentle hold kept her erect on the stool.

When he lifted, he moved slowly, his gaze steady on her. "I love you."

Her mouth went slack. "No, not me. You mean—"

"Yes, honey. *You.*" His thumb stroked down her cheek coming to rest on her chin. He leaned forward, brushing his lips over hers. "I love you, Olivia Matthews." And then he kissed her with so much passion she forgot her name all over again.

Chapter 13

Abe hoisted the garbage bag over his shoulder and dropped it in the dumpster. When the lid banged closed, he rubbed the cold from his bare arms and stomped back into the building, knocking the snow off his sneakers on the soggy hallway mat.

Olivia would be here any minute and he was still pulling the party room together. Even on his worst days he would have been finished ten minutes ago. Then again, a party had never run forty-minutes overtime either.

What a lousy day for a tour.

Abe pushed both garbage bins toward the elevator. He should have given his two-weeks-notice long ago. How could he take Olivia to watch eagles at the Mississippi River if he had to be back by two?

It's about time he quit his kiddy job and grew up. Heck, he was a software engineer, wasn't he? And didn't the church need an app to announce events to those college kids no one else could grab?

With the bins dragging behind him, he stomped out of the elevator and toward the party room. Shoving open the door with his backside, he thrust the bins through. They skidded to a stop on the waxed tile. Perspiration dripped from his hairline and he wiped his brow before opening a cabinet to grab two more garbage bags.

What a lousy—

Olivia stood in the middle of the room, her coat draped over her arm. She still wore the baby blue wrap-around skirt he'd admired earlier in the day, but now she also wore knee-high suede boots and a blue hair bow.

It was hard to believe she could be more beautiful than a few hours ago. And yet, she was.

"Olivia…" His lips curled up, relishing the sound of her name in his ears.

Ever since he'd asked Pam how they decided on Ruby's middle name, he enjoyed saying it out loud. *Olivia.* The name meant "peace," referring to the olive leaf the dove brought back to Noah after the flood ended. The very first sign of life. God's promise of a new beginning being fulfilled.

And the meaning fit Olivia's personality. She was peace. She was content with the simple life she had. No bouncing back and forth between ministries. No flying off to another continent when God could speak to her here in the States.

Olivia was settled.

And he loved that about her. He loved her.

She folded her coat on a nearby chair and took a seat, crossing her legs at the knee. "The girls at the desk pointed me to the staircase that led to the biggest party room." Her eyes drifted to a blue streamer that dangled from the ceiling. "This is definitely it."

He grinned and straightened, snapping the garbage bag open. "Only on Saturdays. During weekdays, this is the preschool room." He cocked his head to the mural of sea animals.

"How was the party?"

"Nuts. The party host ditched when he saw me walk in, so I was on my own."

"Oh boy."

"Exactly what I said." He pulled a bin toward a table and grasped the edge of the soiled cloth, rolling it into a wad. "Turns out the mom brought her own table cloth, plates, decorations. Everything the party host had done, I had to redo, and *then some.* Since we normally *don't* have tablecloths. Or decorations." Abe stuffed the plastic bundle into the bin and punched the garbage down, although he'd already shoved it deep enough.

He heard Olivia giggle and a glance in her direction confirmed his suspicions. Her face was pinched, stifling the sound.

He allowed a chuckle to rumble past his lips as he rolled the bin to the next table. "And—get this. The mom said the bottom of the pizza was doughy. Guess what? All the pizzas are under-baked. What do we look like, a pizzeria?"

Her giggles overcame her and she covered her mouth, her cheeks becoming crimson.

"You think this is *funny?*" Leaving the crumbled tablecloth, he went to the sink to dump a cup of juice. "I find no amusement in my tale of woe."

He couldn't contain the smile that creased his face. Or the heat swelling in his chest as she walked toward him. The brown of her hazel eyes glowed in the fluorescent lights.

"You've been a party host for, what? Six years?"

"Almost seven, but this takes the cake, no pun intended. See this? I'm sweating." He rested his hands on her waist— then sprang back, his eyes on her hips. The fabric of her dress now smudged with red and blue marks. Impressions from his stained fingerprints.

"Sorry, I…"

She gave him a peck on the lips. "It's okay, really."

"It's really not." The vanilla-lavender scent of her shampoo wafted into his nose as she stepped close. His heart pounded in his chest. "As soon as you get home, put some detergent on it. But it looks like it's dry-clean-only, so—"

Her lips covered his, prodding slowly.

He flexed his knuckles at his side. It was all he could do to not run his fingers through her hair. Take her face in his hands and promise her the moon.

"Olivia…"

Careful to keep his fingertips off her skin, he extended the kiss. The confession from the day before came to mind and bore repeating. "Olivia, I love you."

She shuddered, breaking contact. Then she took a step back—away from him.

The breath caught in his lungs. The similarity couldn't be denied. Shying away right after he admitted his love for her, stepping back at the moment of intimacy.

The air of the room seemed to be sucked into the vents and he couldn't catch his breath. A block settled onto his chest.

But this wasn't Ruby. This was Olivia, who just yesterday had believed his love for her. Who had relaxed in his arms and admitted she had feelings for him too.

And Abe had come too far to give up now.

He took her hands, pressing the stained pads of his fingertips onto her palms, not caring if the food coloring seeped into her pores. "Did I scare you? Is that it? Please tell me." Suddenly worried he was being demanding, he gentled his hold on her and softened his voice. "What's the matter?"

Her eyes flickered to his face, worry lines crossed her forehead. "I know you love me, but..." She gave a wobbly smile and darted her eyes away.

A crosshatch developed in between her eyebrows as she studied the painted seahorses.

But. A word that should never be pegged to the end of *"I know you love me."*

As much as he wanted her to open up to him so they could restore their relationship, another part of him was slowly dying. Because she hadn't responded with a *"I love you too"*—a fact that stuck out like the stain on her dress.

Chapter 14

Abe returned to the table and attacked the corners of the table cloth, punching the folds over each other. The block in his gut froze over, hardening to solid ice.

With barely a glance, he regarded the smile Olivia had pasted on her face—phony, all of it. The excuses, her barely concealed irritation with him. He heard it now, in her soft voice. "I know you love me, but what about everyone else?"

"Everyone else? What does that have to do with you and me?" *If you don't feel loved by me, just say it.* He shoved the stack of used cake plates in the trash and kicked a chair out from under the table, landing hard in the seat.

He hunched his shoulders, letting his stained fingers hang between the knees.

Was it his response to her kiss? Too aggressive, too fast? Or had it been the confession?

Whatever it was, he couldn't get this right. He lacked the skill to communicate love. He either waited too long—or spoke too soon.

"Everyone at church knows Ruby, but..." Her voice wavered and got lost in the hum of the radiator.

He craned his neck to look at her but wish he hadn't. The corner of her left eyebrow had dipped, the tell-tale sign she was thinking of something serious. An expression he knew all too well.

His cheeks burned and he exhaled out his mouth. Ruby had asked for time, for space, and he gave to her. And waited. But if he would have known it was a prelude to leaving him permanently, he never would have let her go.

He clenched his fists and shot out of the chair. "You found another church then? I know I said it would be hard for me to leave my church, my spiritual family, but I would do it." His temples pounded, the muscles in his shoulders tightened. Hot moisture welled in his eyes. "I'd do it for you. For us. I love you, Olivia."

She took a deep breath, her eyes steady on him. "Wasn't Ruby baptized as a teenager?"

A tear fell from his eye and he wiped it away with the back of his hand. A chisel had started at his heart. It had been hard enough to get dumped the first time. After this, would he risk loving again?

He leaned his head back, yielding to the pain, releasing the chipped away pieces to his Heavenly Father, who would never abandon him, never leave.

He gave a slow nod. "Yes, as a teenager."

The radiator shut off, giving way to the sound of wind rattling the windows. A drip landed in the sink from the ancient faucet.

Drip… Drip… Drip…

Abe swallowed past the lump. *Just make it quick.*

She pressed her lips together, her chin trembling. "Would it be dumb if *Olivia* was baptized?"

He let the words settle. He tilted his head, narrowing his eyes. "You want to be baptized?"

She lowered her gaze, wiping her cheeks. "I was trying to fit in, to bear with…" The sentence dropped off and he listened carefully for the rest of her thought. "But I have this feeling everyone is always expecting someone else."

A shiver racked her body and she wrapped her arms around her middle. Perhaps her attempt to keep out the draft that came from inside.

The pressure released from his chest and his heart started to beat.

She sniffed, her eyes fixed to the floor. "Baptism is for a new believer and even though I can't remember, I know I'm saved through faith in Jesus, so the ceremony isn't necessary. It's not like I need to publicly announce my faith. I just thought maybe..."

Air filled Abe's lungs. While he had worried that she was pulling away, she had been searching for a way to stay close. He shifted his weight, his gaze steady on her. "You want the church to pray for you? To share with them your story of amnesia, your decision to change your name?"

She nodded. "I don't know what else to do."

The mass in his gut thawed to a puddle.

Olivia...

He stepped to her side and caressed her cheek, careful to use his knuckle and keep his stained fingers away from her skin.

The tsunami of emotion she had been harboring for weeks spilled onto her cheeks. And what of the pressure he had put on her? His impatience when she was tortured on Sundays and adamant hesitation to attend another church? Not seeing her private struggle, but instead assuming her conflict was because she couldn't trust him. He had made her just as uncomfortable as the tight squeezes she was given without warning.

He itched to hold her, to comb his hand through her hair— but he didn't dare. Not unless he wanted streaks of food dye on her backside too.

Years of loving his next-door neighbor had accumulated to this moment. After so much time praying and waiting and hoping, he'd found his chance to prove his love for her.

The corner of his lip twitched as he leaned close and lowered his voice to a hush. "I've been praying for you to find your way into the church community. Being re-baptized is just the ticket."

All at once her face softened. She looked at him through a glass of tears. "You think so?"

He let his face break into a smile. "Honey, it's a great idea."

She squealed and collapsed in his arms, squeezing him around the torso. His breath hitched and he inched back. "Careful—I have icing all over my shirt."

But her fists clenched the back of his polo and she buried her chin in his chest. "To feel like I belong. Everyone at church knows Ruby, but no one knows *me*, Olivia."

"Olivia." He pushed against her shoulders with the balls of his hands but she was clinging to him too tight. "Your dress will be ruined."

"But it wasn't fair to make you leave your church. And where you are is where I want to stay."

"Oliv—Wait. What did you say?"

She took a step back to look at him. "I want to stay." The color returned to her cheeks and she tucked her chin. "But not with assumptions and awkward conversations. It's fine everyone has a story about what Ruby would have said, how she would have acted. But that's all people talk about. Ruby this, Ruby that. Maybe if they heard my story, they could greet me—me, Olivia—on Sunday."

The buzz spiraled down his arms and to his feet. *"I want to stay."* Her words penetrated deep, a healing balm after feeling pushed away, of believing he wasn't able to love, of not being trustworthy enough to deserve commitment. A phrase he hadn't even dreamed of hearing came from the lips of the love of his life. Olivia chose to stay. Not only return to him, but to also remain. Every cell of his body pulsed, seeping life back into his bones.

Right here and now he could commit to a lifetime with her. With his stained fingertips and her ruined dress.

He chuckled, the warmth tickling his belly. "Sounds like you want the church to meet Olivia."

She tugged at a streamer. The tape gave way and the blue

crepe paper twirled to the floor. "I still have to tell Tom—I mean, my dad."

Abe touched her wrist, the corners of his lips inching up. "Tom. One step at a time."

A smile lit up her face, the one that crinkled the corners of her eyes.

She scooped to nab the streamer and crumpled it in her hand. A decoration that had served its purpose and was no longer needed.

The woman he had grown up with, who had copied his notes in high school, who'd begged him to participate in the Easter skit so it wouldn't be canceled and later would break his heart in her parents' dining room now was forced to start over.

But maybe from here, from this new beginning she could find herself. She could finally become the woman he had loved from the start.

Yes, one step at a time.

As Olivia took up the broom, he collected plates, his cheeks aching from the wide smile he couldn't contain. That sense he first felt after his father passed away, when the Holy Spirit had filled him with conviction, when the darkness had split and Christ had taken his hand and led him into an eternal relationship with Him. That same joy and hope filled Abe in that moment. *"Your word is a light for my feet."* *Thank You, Father. Thank You.*

Chapter 15

A cardinal called from a tree outside Olivia's window. She squinted and rolled to a sitting position, wiping the sleep from her eyes. How could she have slept in? The day of her baptism, when she publicly announces—again—her decision to be a part of God's family, to commit to the Lordship of Christ.

Olivia unraveled the sheets, but before she made it to the door to get ready for the day, she noticed a notification on her phone. She touched the screen.

Abe: Good morning, beautiful.

The corners of her lips lifted and she sank back onto the edge of the bed. He had sent the text twenty minutes ago. Was she so late getting ready? Abe and his mom would bring breakfast soon—and she had a million things to do until then!

Olivia: I'm half-awake ;) But I'll be ready soon.
Abe: Better hurry. We're bringing breakfast :)

Bet it's frittata. Whenever she had a big event coming up, she went easy on the carbs and heavy on the protein. Mainly bacon and eggs. And Abe's mom made the *best* frittata.

She wanted to read her testimony over before her baptism ceremony after church. Would there be time in between? Or maybe Abe could... She squinted at the phone as his new text flashed across the screen.

> Abe: You'll never guess what it is.

Olivia rolled her eyes. *Not now, Abe.* She keyed out a message as she headed to the bathroom.

> Olivia: Could I read my testimony to you one more time after church? Think there's time?
> Abe: Yes and yes :)

As she cleaned her teeth, a warmth filled her insides. Always eager to support her. So generous, as if he had been waiting for an opportunity to share his love for her.
Her heart gave a flip-flop.
But now wasn't the time to be sentimental. So much to do! Her phone dinged.

> Abe: I'll give you a hint. It's round, but isn't a pancake.

She lifted her eyebrows. Instead of replying, she took up her hairbrush.

> Abe: An egg dish, but not an omelet.

She retreated back to the bedroom, shaking her head. Didn't he have to get ready too? Didn't he know *she* had to get ready?
Abandoning her phone on the desk, she took the hanger from her closet of the long-sleeved yellow dress she had chosen for today. Yellow because… Well, why not? And she favored the soft feel of the cotton. Seemed so airy and bright. Clean and new.
She got ready for the day in record time, pulling her hair back from her nape into a loose bun and fixing a yellow ribbon flower off-centered. Old-fashioned for sure, but it complemented her complexion. She seemed younger, her skin

softer, so the ribbon stayed.

She was applying gloss to her lips when Abe texted.

Abe: Give up?

Olivia planted a hand on her hip. *Is he serious?*

She could almost smell the bacon now. The hint of oregano and basil—

Abe: Too late. We're here :)

Her cheeks warmed. *That's* why the aroma was so strong.

Enough blabbering! Time to get a move on!

Unzipping the Bible cover, she sifted through papers. Hadn't she put her testimony with her Bible? Where else…?

A thick envelope fell out, scattering its contents. She crouched down, fingering the notes she had written while in Asana. Several photos from her time there. Brother Olatunbi outside the maternity house. Sister Ibanibo, leaning over a bed of hot coals, preparing to make a poultice.

Olivia wiped away a stray tear. She missed the singing. Always a hymn on the woman's lips, even as a pregnant woman underwent the hardest parts of labor.

Her heart thumped in her chest.

Nigeria.

Frittata.

A smile lifted Olivia's cheeks. Praise the Lord. *She remembered.*

Chapter 16

Ruby bounded down the stairs, her bare feet trying to keep up with her pace on the slick hardwood steps.

"Hello, sunshine."

She slammed to a halt as Abe leaned back against the banister, one foot propped on the bottom stair. He wore his usual black sports jacket and pants and his favorite tie. Red with black stripes.

"Abe, you won't believe—"

"Frittata. We brought frittata."

"Yes, yes, I know. Listen—"

"Olivia?" He took a tendril of her hair that had escaped the bun.

She grinned. "You don't have to call me—"

"You look stunning today." His eyes landed on hers, his head cocked to the side. "Full of the Holy Spirit perhaps? Ready for the big day?"

A lump landed in her gut. Big day... Referring to Olivia's baptism... Which wouldn't be necessary, since—

Abe touched his lips to hers. When he lifted, his voice was soft. "Don't be nervous, sweetheart. Remember, I'm rooting for you."

"Yes, well..." She laughed, a bit too high-pitch. All that nervous energy tying her tongue in knots.

He gazed into her eyes, a translucent shine over the muted

browns. The corner of his lip tipped up and his fingertips touched her cheek. "I've prayed for you a million times last night into this morning." His breath against her ear. "I'm so proud of you."

A shiver found its way up her spine. *Proud of me? Or proud of Olivia?*

The way he looked at her, how his eyes kept on her face with a blazing desire was almost as if…

But, no, it couldn't be.

When had Abe ever been proud of her before the accident? Every other moment, he had been in a daze, trying to keep up with her antics. Especially near the end, before she decided to break the engagement to test the waters of love in another's arms, Abe had been downright annoyed at her.

And he'd admitted as much not long ago. She remembered that too. Just last night, on his parent's couch, watching a sitcom on mute. He'd said Ruby would think watching television was a waste of time.

Ruby stepped back, so she could see into Abe's eyes.

Would he be happy to learn she was back? That innocent Olivia who could only live in the present was gone? The way he smiled at her now, caressed her cheek. The way Abe was looking at her, with all that passion in his eyes. So much admiration there.

The drum beat of her heart picked up a notch. The way he spent time in her eyes was the spark she had been looking for. *This* had always been the way she wanted Abe to love her. To feel special by him.

Here it was, in her best friend—and directed at her. Except, not at *her*.

Ruby pressed her hand to Abe's clean-shaven cheek, letting the warmth of his flesh seep into her palm. His Adam's apple bobbed.

She leaned up, letting his hunger drive the kiss and satiate the desire she had longed to quench for so long.

And if he loved sweet Olivia more than her, than the

clothes stored under her bed could find a closet of a different owner. She wouldn't be needing them anymore.

"So…" She ended the kiss to look into the half-moons of his eyes. She let a soft laugh gurgle from her insides, lift her countenance. "Frittata? But why?"

His eyes danced. He touched the small of her back to lead her to the kitchen as he recounted their first choir concert at church in the sixth grade, and how she had been so excited his mom had volunteered to make a breakfast heavy on the protein, just for her.

And Ruby listened, drinking in the attention Abe gave her. She lived in the moment, letting the memory wash over her as if she only heard of it for the first time today. As if she was content with nothing more than Abe's presence.

Restless Ruby was no more. Starting today, she was a new creation. She would be the sweet, peaceful Olivia. What choice did she have? If Abe loved Olivia, Ruby had no home here.

Chapter 17

The trickle of the holy water on Olivia's forehead gave way to streaming tears as the final members of the church came to shake her hand and welcome her to the family of God. Indeed! She had never felt so loved, so important before. She truly didn't need to go across the Atlantic to find herself—because she found it here, in those who cared for her so much. Almost the entire congregation had stayed after church to witness her baptism.

Abe lingered at the side pews. Waiting.

Olivia wiped her eyes and released an even breath. If Ruby reminded herself her name was *Olivia,* meaning peace, rushing shouldn't come naturally to her.

But in reality she wanted to hurry. And get into the line for fried chicken. Because the feast was for her—and she wanted to catch up with everyone over drumsticks and coleslaw.

They *were* looking for her, weren't they? Probably Olivia wouldn't worry about that—Abe certainly wasn't.

He came to stand in front of her, a small smile on his lips. More pride in his eyes than he could hold. "For not having time for a final run-through, your testimony was outstanding. Like it flowed from you."

And it had. As she shared the confusion after the accident, and then the longing to belong, she realized she related to Olivia more than she had realized. It had been her struggle before the accident, but Olivia had made peace with it. She had found a way. And in so doing, found a way for Ruby to finally rest.

She let the smile crease her face. "It was such a blessing. Thank you for—" Her breath caught. Meaning to carry on the charade, she was about to thank him for all his continual support when she realized all she was about to say was true for Ruby too.

She tipped her chin to meet his eyes. "I mean, thank you for everything. For being there for me all this time, even when it was hard and I was confused. Thank you for never abandoning me. You had always been…"

Right there. Not just every day while she was in the hospital and then in recovery, but before that. When she had been dating guys and had pushed him away, seeing the pain in Abe's eyes. Yet, he had always remained on her side, never straying, never distancing himself, even if it hurt to see her fight against him.

He had committed to her and he had kept that promise. Not because he was obligated, but because his love ran deep.

Ruby's throat tightened. She had so much else to tell him, how grateful she had been.

"Sweet Olivia." He cradled her cheek, stroking away a tear as it snaked down her face. "The faucet has been on all day, huh? Must be refreshing after so long."

Was he thinking of Ruby again? That she never gave in to crying, that she would busy herself until the emotion faded. Because she had been afraid to share the depths of her fears and doubts.

But what if Abe really had loved her, as he had said to her many times? Words she never could believe. Could it be her doubts had tricked her? And all the patience her parents had with her as she wandered, changed her mind, and left them to pursue her heart's desires… Was it because they loved her? Truly?

And what of God? She had avoided reading the testimony

again with Abe because she was afraid that her conscience would prick her and she would foil her plan before she attempted it.

But during the service, she committed to leaning on God. That today's baptism wasn't a lie, but was a reinstatement between her and God, a re-commitment to put her life under Christ. This time she desired peace. The peace Olivia had and Ruby wanted for herself.

She had begged God to bless the ceremony—and He had. Two-fold. First by making Olivia's testimony her own. And second when Ruby had unleashed her emotion, she finally broke free from her fears and began to appreciate Abe's love for her. A love she couldn't feel, she couldn't hold but existed.

Abe's hand remained on her cheek, his thumb lightly stroking her chin. And his eyes were on her—on *her*.

Would she ever get used to this? Part of her never wanted to. Instead, she wanted to revel in his attention. To know he cared for her deeply, to believe it.

But then she remembered he was looking at Olivia. He loved Olivia.

The thought hooked into her heart.

What if she had been right all along? What if they had been words only and her assumption was right? That no one loved her. That Ruby wasn't worthy of being loved.

He cocked his head, giving a crooked smile he reserved for skipping gym class. "Let's get our coats."

"But aren't they waiting for me to…?"

He took her hand and led her to the pew where their coats had been heaped. "There'll be plenty of chicken when we get back." He opened her coat toward her and she stepped into it.

He was being kind to shy Olivia, but it irked her. If she didn't get to the basement, how could she be there when someone needed a hand? What if she lost her chance to be helpful?

And her stomach was already growling, not able to finish her slice of frittata as she tried to stay chipper and not rattle off a hundred complaints as her mother bubbled about with more excitement than necessary. If Olivia wanted more orange juice she could help herself, thank you very much.

But if she hadn't reined in her tongue everyone would have known Ruby was back.

And she wasn't ready to go back—not when she was just beginning to feel loved.

Settling her earmuffs around the bun that had been little by little coming loose, Abe gave her another whimsical smile. An expression she hadn't seen since they were kids and it warmed her through. He was comfortable with her. Enjoyed her presence. Who wouldn't? Olivia was a joy.

She matched his slow footfalls toward the arching doors of the church until Abe stopped at the closed door, one gloved hand against the heavy metal handle. The pause continued— what was he waiting for?

And then she realized Abe hadn't been waiting. He had been looking at her, *enjoying* her presence.

Olivia, be still. She drew in a steady breath. *Live in the moment.*

He squeezed her fingers, pulling her closer to him. "Ready?"

She let her head bob, but not too eagerly. Not as if she wanted to get this over with. *Enjoy his presence.*

He pushed the door open and an icy wind blew against her face. She shivered, huddling close to Abe as he stepped through.

Her flats sank into the inch of snow. *Rats! My ankles are freez—*

Her breath caught in her throat. A fresh snow had fallen, coating the pavement with a clean sheet of white, glistening in the sunrays.

She cupped her mouth.

"Amazing, isn't it?" Abe's hands settled on her hips as he came to stand directly behind her, flush against her back. He spoke in a hush, the words drifting around her, carried by a gentle breeze. "It started snowing while you were sharing your testimony. Seemed significant."

With him behind her, she couldn't see his expression—and couldn't be distracted. Nothing blocked her view of the sight in front of her. This brilliant, white masterpiece. To show her what he wanted her to see. To remind her he was thinking of her, that he loved her.

To remind her of God's love too. God's unconditional love she could count on. That she could trust him.

The tears had started again, the winter wonderland swimming in front of her. She sank against his chest. "I've never seen anything like this."

"You have." His hands released to rest on her shoulders, as if fixing her in place. "You just can't remember."

But she *could* remember. And she knew Ruby had never seen snow like this. Had never stopped in her tracks to take in a landscape.

Here and now, snow wasn't the means to slow her down. It was the reason to slow down.

"So… You like it?"

She nodded. Even if she tried, her throat was tight and no words would come. *Abe, thank you. You'll never know how much.*

But his words from an earlier conversation, a stream of consciousness he never would have thought Ruby would hear, came to her mind. And with it a dull ache in her chest. *"Ruby would never have been able to sit long enough to love this."*

And he was right.

Even now there were people she wanted to talk to. Tasks she would rather accomplish. Her feet were ready to turn on her heel and dash back inside.

She closed her eyes to the beauty. *Lord, please make me Olivia. Make me new!*

Chapter 18

Ruby had gone to bed hours before, but still lay awake in her bed, staring at her ceiling of yellow from the last time her favorite color had been the obnoxious hue. She'd been oscillating ever since, and today was no different.

She was finished with yellow. She preferred midnight blue now, so dark and menacing it was one shade from total blackness.

She rolled to her side and nestled her cheek into her pillow. After their trip outdoors, the fried chicken and mingling hadn't been the same. Olivia would have kept to Abe's side, shy and observant. But Ruby wanted to ask questions, to find out what needed to be done and to help.

Why couldn't she be at peace? Why did she need to move constantly? Hadn't God promised to make her new? Wasn't He King? Hadn't He, in His authority and power, given her confidence while she shared her testimony publicly? Hadn't God approved of her decision to recommit?

Then why had she gotten progressively more uneasy as the day drew on? Thank goodness Abe would be at work for the better part of tomorrow, but what about the evening? How was she going to keep up the farce of being content—when she was anything but?

She climbed out of bed and took the two steps to the window. The streetlight cast an eerie sheen on the bare branches of the maple tree. Only stubs of peeling bark with a thin strip of remaining snow. Without leaves, the tree seemed straggly and prickly.

After the mishap with the shawl several weeks ago and Olivia's genuine curiosity, Abe had opened up to her. Drawn close. And Olivia had been so sweet and inviting that he'd kissed her with a passion and hunger she'd never experienced before. Their relationship had never been dry, but it had never had the spark that Olivia and Abe had shared.

Could Ruby really be as sweet and warm as Olivia had been, so Abe would look into her eyes like he was lost in her hazel depths? That he was an explorer with so much to learn, to see, to try?

He'd become awakened by Olivia's fresh look of things. Her appreciation of Abe's love for her.

After a full day of trying to put Restless Ruby in a box and now suffering in moody silence, how much longer could she last? Or was it best to tell Abe and let him go?

Ruby touched the cold glass. As much as Abe said he loved her, he loved someone who was like Olivia. And that wasn't her.

Her breath steamed the window and she used her thumb pad to make a streak through it. Ruby wanted something more. More adventure, more variety. She moved fast and needed freedom to do it. When she was never content, never happy, Abe had become stressed and nervous. He never knew how to please her and so he didn't.

Ruby squinted into the fogged image of the tree branches. The only question was how to stop loving Abe enough to leave for good.

Ruby rearranged her socks in the luggage for the fiftieth time. With nothing else to pack, she had run out of things to do. And the train wasn't leaving for another hour.

"Abe will be home from work in twenty minutes. Couldn't you wait for him at least?"

Ruby looked at her mother and gave a small smile, even though her insides were gnawing at her, eager to get out of the house already. To slam the luggage shut and walk away. She tried to use her sweetest voice. "I'll be back in two weeks."

The woman wrung her hands in front of her. If Ruby couldn't figure out this thing, she'd be as stressed as her mother. Then again, she had never given her mother a carefree ride, had she? As soon as life settled, Ruby would jump ship. Try something new. And her mother was left to worry and wonder.

"Uncle Bert will pick you up from the train station, so you don't need a taxi."

Ruby nodded.

But she intended to stay with her cousins only a day and then strike out on her own. She had plenty of savings, but a job would be in order. After a few nights in a hotel, she'd put down a deposit for an apartment.

By the time Abe realized she wasn't coming back, Ruby—because it would be Ruby again—would have already set down roots three states away. A safe distance where she couldn't see his torn heart. And he couldn't stop her from spreading her wings and taking flight.

"I love you, Ru—Olivia."

Ruby zippered her bag and set it upright. "Love you too." She gave her mother a brief hug, scooted past her, and took the stairs.

Her dad patted her back and gave his typical smile. Whereas her mother worried, her father prayed. He probably had more hold of her than anyone, because how far could she get when someone was tugging her spiritual chords the entire journey?

She wished she could tell her father the truth, but it would have to wait. She couldn't risk her father praying something crazy, like the train to be delayed and her trip canceled. If someone wanted a miracle, he would come to her dad. But if someone was a prodigal daughter, her lips would have to stay sealed.

Ruby gave her dad a final wave before ducking into the passenger seat. On the way to the train station, her mother reminded her a dozen times to call when she arrived in Denver. And she would—by using her relatives' phone. Because by then she'd have changed her cell number.

Oh, she would let her parents know her new number, but under the strict condition they could never give it to Abe.

Her eyes moistened at the thought. Never again to hear his voice. No longer to walk one door down to complain about life and know he was there for her.

But it was for the best. As much as everyone longed for Ruby to return, it would be better if they believed she was still Olivia, who happened to fall in love with the Rocky Mountains.

Abe would get it. Her scant memory had been hard on him too. He had turned a new page when he had gotten the programming job and there were new chapters to be written. Ruby never belonged to those pages.

Besides, she had her own story to write.

She recognized the elementary school. The library, post office, grocery store, and strip mall. All those memories, the history. And then the familiar gave way to the unfamiliar on their way to Naperville.

Goosebumps prickled her arms. This was the first time a new destination didn't give her a burst of excitement and joy. All she felt was sadness. *The old has gone...*

Chapter 19

Abe unwrapped the scarf from his neck and tossed it in the passenger seat. He still wasn't used to the thirty-minute commute when he hadn't gone further than ten miles from home in the past two decades.

Scratch that. He went to Vacation Bible School at Lake Geneva as a kid and that was way more than fifty miles away. He had also peed in his pants the first summer away, but he had stayed the entire week, which was more than some other third graders.

Abe chuckled to himself at the memory.

He had tackled the obstacle course alongside his classmates and lost by a hair to Ruby. She'd never let him live it down either. Losing to a *girl*. He had teased her that he let her win, but they both knew the truth. She was faster than him. And more resilient and more courageous and a hundred other things too.

Traffic became heavy and he gave himself extra reaction time on the highway.

And that's the first thing he noticed when she raced down the stairs yesterday morning. Her spunk had returned. All her reservations had flown out the window—which could only mean one thing.

He refused to let her get a word in edgewise. What would he say? "Of course I know you're Ruby again, silly. I'd recognize you anywhere."

Okay, he hadn't been fair. But before she became too crazy, making up for the last couple of months she'd missed at youth ministry and tossing out her cute dresses for her faded T-shirts, he needed to get her attention. Because this might be the only chance he would ever get for her to listen.

Construction blocked the right lane and he merged to the left.

He had wondered if she would cancel the baptism at the last minute, but she didn't. And then he had waited while she took her place at the pulpit with her two-page testimony in hand. He hadn't lied when he noticed the sunlight pour in through the window and pinpricks of shadows dance near the ceiling. The sky had opened, not cloudy enough to be overcast, but enough precipitation to have snowfall.

It was as unique as Ruby's testimony. It was *her* testimony. And she testified that she decided to recommit to the body of Christ because she was a new creation.

Traffic slowed to a crawl. All he could do was wait. And think, which probably was a good idea, since he had to get to Ruby's by seven to get to the nature preserve on time and give her another nudge to listen to God's voice. By the looks of things, he would make it right on time.

Ever since Ruby's testimony, he'd been thinking of ways to prove to her that she was still Olivia. With more charisma perhaps, but Ruby also had appreciation for the beautiful. For the radiant. Except she never recognized such things as important.

But he needed her to see because if she was always focused on the *doing* and not on the *being* she would miss out on what mattered most. She would always be proving her worth rather than experiencing how much God valued her. How her relationship with God trumped any achievement.

And not just God. How deeply and madly Abe loved this eccentric Ruby. He had ached to see how disturbed she was most of the time, all while she was doing good things for God.

Someday she would get to the end of the road when she no longer could do anything or wasn't needed or ran out of ideas. Then who would she be? Or what if she made a mistake and couldn't backtrack? What then?

If her achievements were the only way to define her identity, she might not be able to bounce back. Abe loved her for too long to let that happen.

The number to their landline appeared on the dashboard and he answered the call. "Hi, Mom. Sorry, I'll be later than usual coming home." He sighed and eased on the brake when the car in front of him came to a full halt, surrounded by slush, snow drifts, and orange cones.

"Oh, is traffic bad?"

"Construction."

She gave a snort. "Say no more."

"So, what's up?"

"I just got off the phone with Tom. Seems that Olivia and Pam are on their way to the train station."

Abe's hands tightened on the steering wheel. *Ruby left?* He had considered she would feel pressed—but twenty-four hours?

"Tom says she'll only be visiting her cousins for two weeks and will be back before Valentine's Day."

His chest deflated. *She isn't coming back.*

He had known she would run away, but he hadn't expected so soon. He pressed his lips together, shifting gears mentally. There was more he had planned to say, more parts to move into place... And now he didn't have the most important piece of all if Ruby succeeded in getting on that train. Nothing he could say over the phone would persuade her—if she hadn't disconnected her phone already.

"Hey, Mom, I gotta go. If I can get off at this—"

"Okay, Abe. Be safe."

He turned his signal on and inched forward, steering toward the shoulder. When he hit gravel, he gunned the engine and raced to the off ramp.

Ruby's reaction outside the church had been priceless. Just as he had prayed and hoped. And he knew it was hard, but he also knew she was never supposed to be only Olivia, who marveled over every little thing. She was Ruby who had more visions than even she could count, where the moon wasn't far enough, the seas weren't dangerous enough, and the scope of the Grand Canyon wasn't wide enough. Ruby could take a dream with both hands—but she needed security in her identity in God to see through to the long-haul.

Come on, Ruby. Don't leave—not again.

Ever since she broke off the engagement—and maybe a few days before that when she tried to avoid him—he'd noticed Ruby had become different somehow. He'd been bothered by the change, annoyed even, but he couldn't figure out what had happened. As if she'd been drifting away for a while and suddenly took a flying leap away from him.

That is, until she wanted to be called by her middle name. The nudge had started then, a gradual understanding to her deepest struggle.

She hadn't been so much as unsettled as she had been unidentified. Not searching for herself as much as she was wandering in the dark, while the shepherd called her name and searched the hills for his missing lamb.

She didn't know she was in the dark. And she didn't know she was lost. She said she was too loved, too sheltered, but for all the love and comforts she had been given, she couldn't reciprocate because she didn't know her family name.

She didn't know her Father. She couldn't recognize His voice.

She *had* at one time. But her sensitivity had become dulled. Weakened. Distant.

He would use his next paycheck to pay for a flight to Colorado if he had to, but he couldn't let her run away. Not when she had already come so far.

Chapter 20

From the counter of traveling brochures, Ruby snuck a glance at the large wall clock. The train was due to the station in one minute. And not a minute too soon. She opened the flap to her purse and took out the ticket. No longer her boarding pass to a twenty-eight-hour train ride, it was the ticket to a new life. Where she would be free to serve whatever ministries she pleased. Where her talents would be appreciated.

And especially where no one would cross his arms and frown at her, as if she couldn't do enough to please him.

Then why did the granola bar land like bits of gravel in her stomach? Why did her fingers tremble on the ticket instead of sending a rush of adrenaline through her?

The image of the lone painting in her family's corridor came to mind. A piece of art her mother had purchased from a Christian artist online, Roth-something, a week before the accident. Inky blue waves crashed on the shore while a white stone lighthouse stood at the cliff, the eyes immediately attracted to the golden window, beaming its light.

Maybe Ruby thought of it now because she'd been free to travel lots of times before, but the harbor had always stayed within sight, beckoning her, welcoming her back. This time she left with the intention of never returning.

A whistle blew outside, long and shrill, announcing the train's arrival. She grabbed her one piece of rolling luggage and stepped into the brisk evening. A strong wind whipped her hair across her face and she pulled her hat further over her ears—right as she spotted a figure beeline toward the platform.

She exhaled sharply. There was a reason why she hadn't waited to say good-bye to him. If her mother asked a hundred questions, her next-door neighbor would ask a million.

Abe bounded across the pavement and stopped abruptly a pace away from her, bending at the waist and cupping his knees, breathing hard. His next sentence came in spurts. "I had to park...a block away...but I made it." He took several breaths, his chest working hard.

"Hi, Abe." Ruby pressed her lips together, mustering her best sweetness. "My cousins invited me to Denver for..." *Think, think.* Then lifted the corners of her lips. "Skiing."

He pressed a hand on her shoulder, void of a glove. His coat was opened and he wasn't even wearing a hat. A line of sweat gathered at his hairline.

Drat. He's going to get pneumonia. She straightened her back. *His own fault, chasing me down!*

He struggled to catch his breath, even as he shook his head and dug his palm into her shoulder. "I'm not letting you get on the train."

"I already..." She lifted her ticket and followed the passenger ahead of her as the line moved. A grimace pulled at her mouth when Abe stepped to her side.

"Ruby, I'm not letting you go." He replaced his hand on her shoulder. "Not this time."

Her jaw dropped, a flutter of butterflies invading her stomach—which she quickly scattered away.

Okay, so he knows. Well, of course he would. Because Olivia wouldn't take an overnight train ride. She'd be scared to death. Especially not after a ceremony that welcomed her into the church family. The last place she would go would be across the country. In the winter, no less.

Yeah, this had Ruby written all over it.

Probably should have thought of a more clever story—too

late now.

Angling her chin up, she glanced at the trickle of passengers boarding the train. In a matter of minutes, she'd be in her seat and traveling west bound. She had wrangled out of her mother's weepy arms unscathed. She could escape Abe's grip too.

Since Abe already knew Ruby was back, the gig was up. She moved two steps to stay in line. "Go away, Abe."

He intercepted her, stepping into her path and planting both hands on her shoulders. "You're running. Usually I give you space, but not today." His eyes were smoldering like that afternoon she broke the engagement. Something burned in their depths. But that couldn't mean…?

Ruby swallowed around the lump in her throat. That look of desire had been reserved for Olivia. He had never gazed at Ruby like that.

Good riddance. The faster she was out of here, the better. For both of them.

"We can have this conversation when I get back." The line moved again and she stepped around Abe to stay with it, her ticket clenched in her gloved hand. Only a dozen people between her and the open doors. She was twenty feet from freedom, if only she could bear the next few minutes.

"Yesterday, Ruby, think. It wasn't Olivia who stepped into the ankle-deep snow."

She tugged on her suitcase, but he was right beside her.

"And it wasn't Olivia who admitted she loved the sight." He spun her around to face him, nearly knocking into the woman standing next in line. "Think about it. It hadn't been Olivia who became speechless."

She shook her head. "Not speechless—"

"Yes, speechless. Admit it, it wasn't Olivia who could only stare, caught up in awe and wonder. Ruby, it was *you.*"

The line had separated from her and a couple of passengers had cut in front. Her cheeks heated. She yanked out of his grip and glared at him. "Yes, it was me. And all I could think about was getting back inside, to talk to someone, to give a friend encouragement. To *do* something. Hospitality is a Christian duty—but you despise me for practicing it!"

Abe's jaw went slack and he backed up an inch. As if she'd slapped him in the face.

She got a better grip on the handle of her luggage and lifted her chin. "I can't pretend to be someone I'm not."

With solid footing, Ruby marched to the train. The stomp of Abe's boot thudded just behind her and she twisted away, bracing herself for the jerk on her shoulders. But her fingers grasped air when Abe stripped the ticket from her hand.

Her blood boiled, poison dripping from her lips as she rounded on him. "That's mine."

"The train leaves without you." With his eyes trained on her, he ripped the ticket in half. Then again. And stuffed the bits of paper in his pocket.

She slammed her fists against her thighs. "You'll be sorry!"

"'God's love has been poured out into our hearts through the Holy Spirit.' You were at church, but were you listening? God says you're loved by Him. 'While we were still sinners, Christ died—'"

"I was listening!" Her stomach squeezed, her head ached. "I know all about God's love, His grace—" Her voice cracked and she looked away, hating the heat finding its way into her eyes. *I tried to be peaceful, but I couldn't do it.*

Tears welled in her eyes and she looked away, toward the entrance to the train. *And you don't love me, so there's no point in staying.*

Inhaling deeply, her eyes cleared enough to see the last few passengers board—but without a ticket, they wouldn't let her on.

And she had nowhere else to run.

Chapter 21

A final whistle sounded as the train quivered, gained momentum and started down the track, leaving Ruby behind. The wind blew, spitting cold on her face, but her eyes were fixed on the engine as it faded into the night. A chill swept through her.

She let her shoulders sag, taking hold of the luggage, and starting back to the parking lot. "You're my ride, huh?"

"No."

She looked at him, eyebrows raised.

His pink cheeks turned a shade darker. "I mean, yes, I am. But we're not done here." He shoved his hands in his pockets and scraped at the thin layer of snow on the pavement with the toe of his boot. "I'm not driving you home so you can turn your back on this conversation. Not if you still think you're the same person you were a few months ago."

His gaze shifted to her. Like an eagle catches sight of prey, Abe latched on to her eyes and she was pinned.

"That you're still the same unsettled Ruby that spent a month in Nigeria and came back with that too-bright shawl and tea leaves. You were listening yesterday all right, but only for the things you could do for God. Good things. Necessary things. But when your sense of worth is based on your performance…"

"I'm nothing."

She bit her bottom lip. The words slipped out—with more truth than she could have conjured if she had tried. The most vulnerable moment she'd experienced since... Well, she didn't know if she'd ever experienced such transparency before.

"What you do adds up to nothing, that's right. But that's not where your value comes from."

He stepped closer to her and held her upper arms, slight pressure through the layer of fabrics. "You heard it yesterday—don't you remember? It is the person who trusts God who is righteous, not based on works, not based on what we do. Ruby, you're already favored, already loved by God, so much so that Jesus bought you at a price. He laid down his life for you."

"Since we have been justified through faith…"

The words trickled into her conscience, not by her own memory, but by a prompting of Him who resided inside of her. A ruler who sat on the throne of her heart—but who she'd shut out for far too long.

"We have peace with God through our Lord Jesus Christ through whom we have gained access…"

Daughter, you have access to Me.

The voice, the impression in her heart she hadn't heard or felt in years. Tears leaked out her eyes and she couldn't stop them.

"Poured out into our hearts…"

But in Nigeria, she discovered her heart had been sealed shut. Nothing could get out—and nothing could get in.

The platform and surrounding depot were now deserted, except for Ruby and Abe. And his eyes drilled into her, waiting—for what?

Because she *used to be* more open. Before she found how helpful she could be in the church, before her sense of identity was covered up by good deeds for God.

Not intentionally, but she had closed up. Having received instant gratification from humans, she had been filled before she had a chance to sit under the fount of God's love.

"You felt something, didn't you?" Abe's cheeks were becoming chapped in the cold, his ears red and undoubtedly freezing. But heat radiated from his eyes. "Yesterday in the snow? Did God touch a part of your life, something inside, that had been dormant for a long time?"

She blinked, trying to stomp out the emotion but it was overwhelming. That craving, that desire to experience the sensation again. God's touch, the moment of clarity, when she was being motionless and *certain*. The knowledge of who she was created by and for what purpose.

Such importance and value and love had sunk into her heart uninhibited, seeped in without measure from her Creator God and Savior who gave generously, not asking for anything in return but her devotion and gratitude.

A response. Not a requirement.

Her eyes returned to the vacant train tracks. If she had traveled west-bound, she wouldn't be free, would she? She'd still be chained to her need to be useful, enslaved to her addiction for approval.

She had been free at one time. Brand new. Soaring high. When she first met Jesus as a teenager and loved Him—not because of what she could do for Him, but because of what He had already done for her.

Ruby hugged her middle as an ache opened, a gashing wound she hadn't wanted anyone to know about, anyone to see. And especially not the King Himself.

Was that what Abe wanted her to admit? The moment she had lost her way? When she stepped on the path of only being God's servant, and no longer sat on His lap as His daughter?

Yesterday she had lapped up the love God had lavished on her, freely given at a great cost, after being so empty and dry for so long—and then immediately went inside and dumped the contents onto whoever was available, until she had no reserves left.

She hadn't thought to bring the emptiness to her Father

God. As if on Sunday she heard a checklist to what God required, not as God knocking on the locked door of her soul with His abundance, ready and eager to satisfy her deepest need of belonging.

All she had to do was unlock the door and her Father would have come in. No checklist. No good deed required. Her Father God loved her so much He was insistent on giving her tangible evidence. A love that was true and constant, undeserved and unconditional.

"But God demonstrated his own love for us in this: While we were still sinners, Christ died for us."

A gift. Not purchased. Not earned.

She squeezed her belly. Was she willing to do it? Could she stay still long enough for God to do the work for her?

"Ruby..."

The sound soothed her. Her name.

Abe drew her into his arms, even as she shivered against the sudden affection. Affection she hadn't asked for, hadn't done anything to earn.

When he spoke, his voice was layered with sugar. "When I saw how dried out and exhausted it made you to try to please God, it killed me inside. Because you are already valuable in God's sight—and from *that* place God asks you to serve Him. Not before. *Never* before."

Sugary syrup. Coated with caramel and dripping with hot fudge. Heat climbed up her throat, moisture collected in her eyes.

"And that goes for me too. I love you, Ruby—not because of what you do, but because you're you. And I hope you can love me too, not because I demand it, but because you believe it. Because you love me back."

She looked at Abe, red and shivering, probably frozen to the bone. She slid off her hat and the wind tossed her hair, heat lifting off her scalp, sending a shiver down her body as she set it on his head.

"Oh no, you don't." Abe swiped the hat from her hands

and settled it back on her hair. "You're the jewel, the valuable one. And I could stand here all night in the cold and convince you of that."

"I'm not—"

"Not the same worth as a jewel? You're right. You're not. In fact, you're worth *far more* than many rubies." A smile creased his face, twinkling his eyes. "Far more than any gem. Even the foundation of the city, laid with every precious stone available in heaven cannot boast of such value."

A peace evaded her body, soothing the ache. Her value. More precious than the jasper and sapphire, of the agate and emerald of the New Jerusalem, for which she was named. Her parents' eternal hope of the city ruled forever by King Jesus.

Her identity.

Not because of anything she could do for God, but because of what Jesus had already done for her. His ransom for her, a payment made in His own blood.

A smile lifted her lips. She liked the sound of that. Ruby, who is worth far more than many rubies.

She cocked her head, her eyes narrowed. "As far as the fear of God is concerned…"

"That reference to Proverbs thirty-one slipped. Honest. I was only thinking of the city in Revelation."

"But the Proverbs thirty-one woman is my hero."

Abe took her hand, his sigh fogging in front of his face. "Oh, Ruby." He grinned and she fell into step next to him, the rollers of the luggage scraping behind her, the yellow glow of the streetlights guiding their path.

"There was an owl walk tonight."

A giggle started in her belly. "Oh, too bad Olivia missed it."

"Yeah, well, the sighting was never for her anyway." He swung her arm in between them, giving her a side-long glance, his lips curling. "It's followed by a do-it-yourself dissection of an owl pellet. Got your name all over it."

"A freezing walk and breaking open clumped fur have my

name?"

He nodded. "I've got the entire week planned. If Olivia lasted that long."

"Boy, you don't know me at all."

"Guess not." He grinned, stepping in front of her. The liquid chocolate of his irises blazed. "I love you, Ruby. Always have, always will."

Ruby smiled, letting the passion in his expression sink into her conscience, memorizing the sensation that filled her mind, her heart, her soul.

"I know." She reached up, meeting his lips, as if for the first time.

Letter to Reader

This theme has probably been told in more stories and movies than any other. The dilemma of identity, of wondering how a person fits in with her unique gifts, while seeking approval from others.

(The fact that I wrote this story means I struggle with this too!)

Whether you feel accepted or not, the truth is God created you and God loves you. You are intrinsically valuable because of your Maker. If that's not enough to give you chills, God also redeemed you back to Him at a high cost. Because of your sin, you cut yourself off from God, but God forgave your sins through the holy blood of Jesus and brought you back to Him, to enjoy Him, your Creator, your Father, your true husband and your King forever.

This is a love and value that you won't find in the world—but that you desperately desire! And for good reason. We were made to be in a relationship, including godly friendships with sisters in Christ and at church. If you haven't already, reach out to a woman you trust and start praying with her once a month to receive much-needed love and support for your faith journey!

For more support, Nancy Leigh DeMoss Wolgemuth and Anne Graham Lotz have excellent resources for understanding your worth as a daughter of the King.

May you be filled with Jesus' overwhelming grace today and always!

Your sister in Christ,
Cheryl

Discussion Questions

Chapters 1-5
1. Abe struggles to trust God's sovereignty and goodness while he faces a confusing time. Read Matthew 6:26, 30-32. How do these verses comfort you, if you are experiencing a challenging situation today?

Chapters 6-8
2. Olivia took a new name when she had difficulty fitting into her family and church. Read Genesis 17:3-5. What similarities can you find in the reason for Abraham and Olivia taking a new name?

Chapters 9-10
3. Abe needed to confront the more painful moments in his relationship with Ruby to move beyond the grief to a new future. Look at Luke 5:1-11. What opportunities would Simon have missed if he didn't move into the uncomfortable place of obedience to Jesus?

Chapters 11-14
4. Abe confesses his love to Olivia, which ultimately sets him free from his insecurities. Read 1John 4:10. If you have not yet accepted Jesus as your Savior, what does this verse teach you of how Jesus confesses His love to you? If you have a relationship with Jesus, how could confessing your love to Jesus elevate your spiritual life today?

Chapter 15-17

5. Ruby wrestled with herself to be still and have peace with God. Read Romans 5:1. If you could talk to Ruby about her restlessness, how could you use this verse to help her experience peace?

Chapters 18-21

6. Abe tells Ruby that her value doesn't come from what she does for God. If your value doesn't come from the good you are able to do, where does your value come from? (See John 3:16; Romans 5:8; 1Peter 1:18-19)

Acknowledgements

I'd like to thank those who loved me when I was in my Olivia-state, confused and wondering who I am, until I could accept my identity in Jesus Christ.

To Dr. Paul Koh, who has met with me and loved me faithfully with Bible study and a word of encouragement for the last twenty years.

To Dr. Helen Rarick, who listened and bore with me since my early years as a mom, and has included me as a fellow co-worker in Christ.

To Amie Tallacksen, who always finishes phone calls and voicemails with "I love you!" and reminds me that God loves me.

To my writing partners, Michael Jarnebro, Seralynn Lewis, Chandra Blumberg, Jenna Carlson, Candice Yamnitz, who spoke truth in love until God's desire for me became reality.

To my mom, whose love lifts me up and holds me close; to Dad, from whom I've inherited this angst to create; to Ashley who has never failed to support my love for writing; and to Avrey, who looked at me in all earnestness and asked, "What's your book about?"

To Barb Kramarczyk, who called me after reading my first novel and told me my writing was a gift from God.

To Adam, who taught me the enduring, everlasting quality of love in our first year of marriage.

To Barnabas, who reads what I've written over my shoulder, and to Silas, who asks, "When's my turn on the computer?" You are both God's gift to me. XXOO

And to Jesus Christ, who demonstrated His love for me in this: while I was still a sinner, He died for me.

About the Author

Cheryl started writing in 2015 after the birth of her second son. Feeling betrayed and angry that God hadn't kept His promise to her in Psalm 37:4, she started a dialogue with God for the first time.

Along with prayer and Bible reading, she wrote a short novel to see how her characters would persevere in unfair situations. One novel became three, and her heart and mind opened to the love and sovereignty of God, who doesn't give His children the desires of their heart, but gives them the desires of *His* heart, which is eternal, pure and glorious!

In 2019, she was named a finalist for the ACFW-Virginia Crown award and a flash fiction winner in the Spark Flash Fiction spring/summer 2020 writing contest. Currently she is the author of two novellas, *Stay with Me,* and *Return to Me*, and has a four-novel Christian Romance series in the works!

 When she isn't writing and rewriting, you'll find her in a hospital working as a lab tech or enjoying the adventure of homeschooling two sons, ages eight and five, with her husband of fourteen years in Chicago, Illinois.

Want more Christian romance? Grab "Stay with Me" at https://www.cherylkramarczyk.com/free_novella! Cheryl can also be found on…
Facebook: Cheryl Kramarczyk the Author
Twitter: @CAKramarczyk

By the Same Author

She can't risk him learning her secret,
he can't risk losing her.

Penelope Roth has spent the last six months securing plans to merge her father's company with Whitestone Distributors, not to mention falling in love with its CEO, Tucker Caldwell. That is, until she spends time with her aunt and learns of God's purpose for her life. Can she keep her heart intact while working with the handsome entrepreneur—or at least avoid the risk of him learning her devastating secret?

Tucker Caldwell is one interview away from being recognized as leading the most profitable distributor in the Midwest. He still has a chance, even as the lovely daughter of his mentor, Penelope Roth, works behind his back to bankrupt his company. As he appeals to her demands of God-honoring investments, the foster kid in him meets her God who calls him son—but is love worth surrendering the years of achievement he'd managed to save up?

Get your copy of *Stay with Me* by Cheryl Kramarczyk today!

www.ingramcontent.com/pod-product-compliance
Lightning Source LLC
Chambersburg PA
CBHW030641130626
46552CB00002B/962